His kiss [...] tion all at once. It filled her heart with an affirmation of his feelings for her. No man kissed a woman the way he was kissing her unless she meant something to him. Sweet as the kiss was, remnants of her dream left Sabrina wanting so much more. Without breaking the spell, she made a sound, a kind of questioning moan, to communicate what she wanted. A second later, John was exactly where she wanted him to be.

All over her.

More accurately, she was all over him.

Somehow John had lowered them to the floor, his arms still inside the sleeves of the shirt she was wearing, his hands a heated presence pulling her flush against him. His lips tugged and pulled from her a passion she had saved for him alone.

"I need to touch you," he said in a harsh breath.

"You are touching me," Sabrina whispered into his mouth.

"Not where, and definitely not how, I want to."

STORM

PAMELA LEIGH STARR

Genesis Press, Inc.

INDIGO

An imprint of Genesis Press, Inc.
Publishing Company

Genesis Press, Inc.
P.O. Box 101
Columbus, MS 39703

ISBN: 13 DIGIT : 978-1-58571-323-3
ISBN: 10 DIGIT : 1-58571-323-6
Manufactured in the United States of America

First Edition

Visit us at www.genesis-press.com
or call at 1-888-Indigo-1-4-0

DEDICATION

This novel is dedicated to Clydia Austin Giron,
our shelter from the storm.
Thank you for your patience, open heart and open arms.
We can never express the magnitude of our gratitude.

Saturated With Katrina

Everywhere I go,
Someone's life is on the sidewalk
My face curls up,
A flimsy attempt
To prevent
The stench from entering my nostrils
The speech in my periphery
Of losses, lies, dreams halted
In their tracks
Causes my ears to vibrate
A sadness that plunges into my spirit like a torrent wave
My Town! My Town! My Town!
My People! My People! My People!
My mouth curls up
My fingertips warm, in the sweet grip of reunion

By Angela Foy Thomas
My sister and ONE of MANY Hurricane Katrina victims still rising

CHAPTER 1

It was no use.

It was dying.

Dreading the only decision left to her, Sabrina Adams guided the car to the shoulder of the road, moving faster in her sputtering twelve-year-old Corolla than the stalled traffic she'd sat in for the last ten hours. The narrow shoulder was not quite wide enough to accommodate her compact-sized car. Coming to a complete stop partway on the shoulder and partway on the grassy field running parallel, Sabrina threw her car into park, shut the engine off and stared out the windshield as the radiator released its last, fiery breath with a tremendous puff of smoke.

She had been warned that the radiator was on its last leg and that her Band-Aid approach of periodically adding water would one day fail. The radiator needed to be replaced and she had planned on getting it done one day last week.

Which was exactly what she had said the week before. And she had meant it, had even put money aside for that exact purpose, but a more pressing matter had derailed her.

Sabrina got out of the car and stared at the bumper-to-bumper traffic stretching as far as she could see. Thousands were fleeing New Orleans, heading for higher ground.

A hurricane was headed toward New Orleans *again,* and like the year before with Hurricane Ivan, it was a snail-moving-through-molasses evacuation. Nevertheless, people were taking the threat of Hurricane Katrina seriously.

Despite the inconvenience . . .

Despite the traffic . . .

Despite last year's memory of a fifteen to twenty hour drive that would normally take no longer than two to five hours . . .

Katrina could be the one the entire population of New Orleans had been warned about for as long as she could remember, all her life probably. "New Orleans is a bowl," she had heard over and over again. With Lake Ponchartrain to the north of the city and the Mississippi River running through it, if the city got a direct hit there would be no place for the water from the storm surge to go. It was a bit hard to imagine, but who would dare to be stuck in such a situation?

Not her.

Which was why, having a car, slightly handicapped as it was, she was evacuating. A little late, but that couldn't be helped. A steady, constant breeze washed over her, a heavy scent of rain in the air. She needed to find some shelter. According to the radio report the storm would be making landfall in a matter of hours. Pulling her cell phone out of her pocket she dialed her uncle's house for the twenty-fifth time. Her grandmother was safe. She had already been picked up, transported and made comfortable by her uncle who lived in Lafayette, Louisiana, about one hundred forty miles from New Orleans, where she had been headed herself. That is, until she found herself in the wrong lane for the contra-flow designed to help relieve traffic. It had steered her northeast toward Hammond and no one, instead of northwest toward Lafayette and family. If she didn't show up, her grandmother would worry and wouldn't sleep, which would keep her Uncle Darren from sleeping. He needed to sleep, because storm or no storm, he had to go to work the next morning. Uncle Darren was one of Lafayette Police Department's finest. He would be dealing with the influx of people evacuating from New Orleans. There would be thousands of people simply coming through or looking for a safe place to stay for awhile. Sabrina knew from Uncle Darren's muttered complaints during, and just after, last year's mandatory evacuation that dealing with the effects of such a large mass exodus, for even a brief period of time, stretched the resources of all nearby cities and towns.

"Can I help you, ma'am?" A young state trooper mercifully interrupted her rampaging thoughts.

Turning to fully face the officer, Sabrina snapped her cell shut to the recording she had heard over and over again, informing her that she, along with thousands of other customers who were calling their loved ones, could not get through to the party dialed and should try again at a later time.

But *voilá*, she had the next best thing: a handsome state trooper. Well, not exactly handsome, but definitely cute, but nowhere near as cute as John, especially when he—

"Ma'am, can I assist you?"

Pulling in her wayward thoughts, which always ran wild when she was nervous, Sabrina smiled and nodded at the cute trooper who could never compare to John, but who could direct her to the nearest police station or shelter where she could use a phone.

"Your car?"

"It died."

"So I noticed."

"It's the radiator."

The trooper nodded. "Can I give you a lift, get you out of harm's way? The highway is closing as soon as the traffic dies."

"I know. I just made it out a couple of hours before the highways closed in New Orleans."

He nodded again impatiently. He probably thought she was nuts standing in the middle of nowhere conversing on the topic of road closures when she should be jumping at the chance for help. The leery look that crept onto his face confirmed it. But Sabrina wasn't nuts, just worried about her grandmother. She had had a heart attack a few months ago and though mild, the possibility of losing her had scared Sabrina enough to keep her at her grandmother's side until two days ago. At that time she had had no idea that Hurricane Katrina would decide to make her way to New Orleans. The hurricane had been heading to Florida, as most of them did. The only thing that had torn Sabrina away from her grandmother's side was the old woman's insistence that Sabrina celebrate her twenty-first birthday, which was what she had been doing with her best friend Kara. Celebrating her adulthood and her decision to tell John Lewis exactly how she felt about him. That, of course, turned out to be a disaster. She had been so wrapped up in *said disaster* and Kara was so knocked out from lack of sleep due to Sabrina rehashing her most recent embarrassing encounter with John, that Sabrina had not noticed the heavy flow of traffic leaving New Orleans as they headed back into the city. It wasn't until Sabrina pulled into the driveway of her friend's home to find Kara's sister storming down the steps, her arms overflowing with luggage, that she learned of the mandatory evacuation. After leaving Kara to evacuate with her sister, Sabrina raced home to pick up Grammy and a few essentials and begin their own evacuation. However, when she reached home, she found a curt note from Uncle Darren telling her that he had collected Grammy and that she should "call and get your butt to Lafayette ASAP!"

The cutie interrupted her thoughts once again. "Can I escort you to a shelter? I have a few other motorists in your predicament."

"Yes, of course, I'd appreciate that."

Sabrina followed the trooper to a police van, nodding to the handful of passengers as she took a seat. Instead of pulling into the congested highway, the van moved across the field and onto a small dirt road. Sabrina tried to relax against the warm vinyl, assuming that this was some sort of shortcut.

"All this traffic and bother for nothing," a nasty voice said behind her. "Watch, we'll all be back in a day or two, three at the most, having evacuated for no good reason. The hurricanes always miss us. Watch and see."

Sabrina turned to see a middle-aged balding man with a huge belly taking up most of the seat behind her.

"If it wasn't for you I'd be in my own house relaxing with a couple of beers," he told a scrawny blonde women sitting on what was left of the seat. The woman ignored the grouchy man and Sabrina's look of sympathy, staring straight ahead.

"The traffic and the situation have made us all irritated," the trooper was saying, "but in the long run you'll be glad you listened to the authorities and evacuated."

"I doubt it," the man grumbled before falling silent.

Turning away from the disgruntled passenger, Sabrina noticed a frail, elderly man sitting next to a middle-aged one who could be nothing other than his son. She remember seeing them on the highway a few miles back. The sweltering heat of August in southern Louisiana had looked as if it were draining every bit of energy from them as they sat in the barely moving traffic with windows rolled down. Sabrina understood their predicament. Her air conditioning barely functioned, blowing only semi-cool air, but at least she had that much. And she was young to boot. She smiled at them. They mustered a smile of recognition and a quiet hello.

The sight of them brought her grandmother to the forefront of her mind again. Trying to clear her head of worry, Sabrina allowed herself to relive part of her birthday adventure, *only the good part.* After all, it was because of her adventure that her uncle had had to travel to New Orleans to take her grandmother to safety. Because of her adventure, she had left the city just before the highways were closed and long after her grandmother. And it was because of her adventure that she had embarrassed herself more than she had ever done in her life, a major feat in and of itself.

"John." She sighed his name, wallowing in her infatuation. No, not infatuation. Her grandmother thought it was infatuation, and maybe at one time it had been. As a teenager she had sighed and mooned over John Lewis and his identical twin brother Josh every time she saw them and every hour in between. But then, one day she'd found herself mooning over John, and only John. He was somehow the more handsome of the two, even taking into consideration the identical twin thing. John was the one she had fallen in love with.

John, so sweet and talented and probably still completely mortified and mad as hell that I made a pass at him. Sabrina pressed her face into her palms. She lifted her eyes a moment later to stare at the lights of a three-story building that looked like a school, situated on the side of the dark highway. A lone figure was walking toward the building, carrying what looked to be an instrument case. The deceptively slight build, the straight, confident walk . . . It couldn't be him. But as they drove closer Sabrina had no doubt that it was.

It made perfect sense. They had both left from the casino hotel where he had played a gig with his jazz band. John had been loading his car when she and Kara had pulled off. Of course she had avoided him. She couldn't avoid him now. John was walking toward the same shelter where she would probably be spending the next two or three days if the grouchy guy's prediction was right.

Sabrina's heart beat double-time.

She'd get to see him again.

But she didn't want to see him.

She'd feel awkward, but what was new about that?

But then, he'd feel awkward.

Now, that would be new.

Before she could decide how she would deal with the awkwardness that they were both bound to feel, the other passengers were getting out of the van.

Sabrina hopped out behind them, turning in the direction she had seen John walking. She took a deep breath in an attempt to calm her nerves.

"Woman, just what did you pack in this big old suitcase? Don't you know we'll be back in the city as soon as this thing passes?" the loud, rude man yelled at his wife as he hefted the suitcase out of the rear of the van.

"Pictures, important papers and some personal things—"

"I don't know why you packed all that," the man went on as Sabrina turned to catch up to the state trooper.

She reached a hand to his shoulder to get his attention. "I forgot my suitcase in my car. Can we go back?"

"Sorry, ma'am," he turned to say, laying a hand on her shoulder when disappointment took over her face.

"It's after midnight and not safe to be out. Perhaps tomorrow, after the storm has passed."

At that moment Sabrina felt John behind her, his eyes boring into her back. "Shooting for more attention, Pest?" he paused to say before continuing toward the shelter.

No he didn't! Sabrina's worry about any potential awkwardness was dispelled with his words. Her eyes locked onto the firm behind and broad shoulders of the man walking away from her as if he barely knew her, as if he'd never kissed her, as if she had never thrown herself into his arms, pressing her body against his hard chest, savoring the heat and scent of him while her mouth had its way with his. Well, exactly who did Mr. John Lewis think he was! Implying that she was after this cute trooper, who still had a hand on her shoulder. A warm hand that didn't pull the least bit of yearning or excitement through her the way a simple glance from John created overpowering feelings of longing and a heart-pounding thrill at being near him.

"I'll see what I can do about your bag tomorrow, ma'am," the trooper said before heading back to the van.

Life would be so much easier if she could do something as simple as fall for a guy like the trooper. But no, she was destined to find herself panting for Mr. Nose-Up-in-the-Air Lewis.

Panting.

Yes, girl, that's what you've been doing, but not any more. Gusts of wind pushed her toward the shelter doors. The name above them confirmed that the shelter was indeed a school.

You're twenty-one now, not a silly teenager. Act like an adult! She had gone to Mississippi for the purpose of watching John play in a band at one of the casinos. And most importantly, to tell him how she felt about him. Which had pretty much amounted to throwing herself at him, only to be tossed aside.

Gently, but *firmly* tossed aside.

Sabrina grimaced as she remembered exactly how firmly she'd been tossed aside. Entering the well-lit foyer of the school-turned-shelter, she walked down a hall toward the sound of people. In a large gymnasium people clustered in small family groups. Sabrina made her way across the crowed floor, finding a small entrance to the stands that were sparsely occupied. Spotting the elderly man and his son across the gym Sabrina changed directions and walked over toward them.

"Are you two okay? Can I get you anything?"

"What a nice girl," the old man said, barely making it into the folding lounge chair with his son's help.

"That's nice of you," the son said, "but I'm sure you have things you need to do. The director just warned us that the lights would be turned off soon."

"I've just got me to take care of," Sabrina told the man, her heart going out to him. "Just tell me, is there anything I can get for you before I settle in?"

"Some water would be nice," the old man said. "I can't seem to get that parched feel out of my throat after staying in the hot car all day."

"Water coming up!" Sabrina dashed away in search of water, wishing that she had remembered her bag. She'd had a twelve-pack of water and a ton of snacks and fruit. Before she could make it too far, the lights flashed on and off and she heard an announcement.

"Second notice. Lights out, ladies and gentlemen, in five minutes. Remember, we're safe from the storm. Tomorrow will be a new day. We again apologize for the lack of supplies. The Red Cross will be sending in cots and blankets as soon as they can."

People moved about restlessly, settling down for the night. The tension in the air was tinged with the hope that the woman who had made the announcement was right about them being safe. Sabrina glanced over at the younger man, an apology in her eyes as she wondered if she had enough time to catch the woman who was heading down the hall.

"Here you go," John said, slapping a bottle of water into her palm. "You better find a place for yourself before the lights go out. You might end up stepping on somebody, maybe even accidentally cuddling up to someone you don't know."

Before she could respond, he had moved into the bleachers directly above the old man and his son. Sabrina handed the water to the man's son and turned to pick her way across the gym floor, making it into the bleachers on the opposite side just as the lights were flashing for the last time. She stared across the gym at John. He'd stretched his long body across one of the bleacher rows using his backpack as a pillow. He wore a hard, piercing look as the lights went out for the night.

Tired, achy, and disgusted with herself, Sabrina stretched out along the hard bleacher row. This was as comfortable as she was going to get. Her suitcase would have made a wonderful pillow and the blanket she usually kept in the trunk of her car would have added a bit of softness to the hard wooden bleachers, as well as providing a decent layer of protection from whatever might have been left on the surface from the many fans who had sat here.

"Oh well, there are worse things in life," she sighed, knowing that sleeping on the bleachers in a shelter was better than being stranded on a dark highway in the middle of a hurricane. Digging into her pocket, she pulled out her cell phone once again. When she tried to call her uncle's house, she received the same recorded message indicating that the call could not go through. Feeling frustrated and helpless, Sabrina flipped the phone shut but kept the power on. She slipped it back into the pocket of her pants in case her uncle or grandmother tried to call.

Leaning away from the light that filtered in from the foyer, Sabrina didn't expect to sleep. The threat of rain and tropical storm-force winds, even a few hundred miles inland from where the hurricane would make landfall, was very real. Despite her worry for her grandmother and the storm, however, she eventually fell asleep, knowing that even though John had been rude he would make it up to her. He always did. It was because he loved her, too. He just didn't realize it yet.

In the soft light easing into the gym John watched her.

And he noticed.

He noticed her shapely form, though it was a mere outline in the diminished light. He heard a deep sigh from across the gym or maybe he had imagined he had heard it because he could see the way her rounded breast moved with each deep, long breath. Sabrina seemed almost a part of him.

John shook his head!

Rounded breast.

Deep breath.

A part of him?

This was wrong!

All wrong.

He couldn't think of Sabrina like that, not *like a women.* She was "the pest." The little girl who, at one time, was the next door neighbor and sometime babysitter for his sister Ness (short for Vanessa).

But it was too late now. He'd noticed her. She was a woman and she was interested in him. From the way she'd pressed herself against him the night before, he had no doubt about that. This was all so very wrong. He didn't have time for a woman in his life. His career was just taking off. He had landed a temporary spot in a well-known brass jazz band because their trumpet player got busted for drinking and driving and then held for the many parking and speeding tickets in his name. The player's tough break had been a good one for John.

He had tried to let Sabrina down without hurting her feelings. She needed to understand that he wasn't interested in her that way. But now he was coming to understand that he *was* interested in her *that way.* But he didn't want to be, which was why he had been so nasty to her earlier today. That, and the fact that he had been jealous of that trooper, who'd had the nerve to put a hand on her.

His eyes having fully adjusted to the sparse light in the gym, John couldn't keep them off Sabrina as he puzzled over his new feelings for her. Staring at her, he finally noticed a few other important things. She didn't have a thing with her. No blanket, no suitcase, no pillow. Her head lay across one long, outstretched arm. She seemed to be sleeping, but how that was possible he didn't know. He couldn't leave her to sleep in such an uncomfortable position all night long just because he was leery of how she was making him feel. Ness would never forgive him, he told himself, using that excuse to justify the decision he had already made.

John scanned the gym floor, trying to gauge the best way to get to her. The floor was literally littered with sleeping bodies exhausted from the long hours spent on the congested highway. So, going across the gym floor was out. He'd have ended up waking half the people down there. His only other option was to stay in the stands and make his way around to the other side. He would have to make the journey without much light because the far end of the gym was pitch black.

His instrument case in hand and a small backpack on his shoulder, he slowly made his way across to the rounded end of the gym, banging his shins a time or two, hoping he was able to avoid encounters of the sticky kind. Coming around to the side of the stands where Sabrina had settled, John kept his eye on her sleeping form as he got closer and closer, refusing to consider that his decision to make her more comfortable was anything more than an act of kindness from one friend to another.

John stopped a few feet away, taking in the sight of her. She had a dancer's body, which made sense. She was a dancer and at one time had been a gymnast. He remembered her trying to impress him by bragging about her skills. He also remembered her wearing braces and worrying about breaking out if she ate too much chocolate. The memories of a younger Sabrina were all overridden by the sight of her shapely form, perfectly accented in a tank top that hugged her breasts and ended just above the waist of the white Capri pants she wore in deference to the hot August heat. Thankfully, the shelter had an efficient air condition system that gave them all a bit a relief. Wondering if the air was too cool for the tank top she wore, he placed a hand on her shoulder. That was a mistake. She was warm. The soft smoothness of her skin was a contradiction to the firm muscle beneath his hand, gained from her active profession as a dance teacher. Despite the warmth he felt, she shivered beneath his touch. Pulling his hand back, John stared at it as if to extinguish the tingling sensation simply touching her had left behind.

Putting his trumpet case down, he eased the backpack off his shoulders and found one of his cotton button-down shirts. It was the closest thing he had to a blanket. Sitting beside her, trying not to think about the rounded breasts that were now up close and personal, he gently eased her upward until her head rested on his upper thigh. Too late he realized what a mistake that was. Shrugging his shoulders, John was suddenly too tired to do anything about it. The gig, Sabrina throwing herself at him, the sudden mandatory evacuation that he hadn't known about until he was on his way back home, running out of gas and walking a mile to get to this shelter before the storm hit, all the events of the last twenty-four hours had taken their toll.

Using his backpack as a pillow, John drifted to sleep, knowing he had to find a way to deal with Sabrina.

CHAPTER 2

John's eyes sprang open. Immediately, a number of things got his notice.

It was still dark, so morning hadn't come yet.

Sabrina had twisted in her sleep, which positioned her face, and soft breath, mere inches from his groin. A steady warmth penetrated the thin cotton shorts he wore, which had already brought him to an instant hardness and throbbing need with no relief in sight. None with Sabrina, that much was for sure.

He needed to move her, to wake her up. But then again, he wasn't ready for a wide-awake Sabrina.

She moved.

John held his breath, hoping that she'd turn her head in the other direction. Instead, her hand came up to rest under her cheek, the tips of her fingers grazing the crease where his thigh and hip met. Drawing a deep breath between his teeth, John released it in slow, steady puffs. Sabina was making him crazy. Even while she slept, she was making him crazy.

He definitely needed to do something about her. When this whole hurricane situation was over with, when they were back home in their normal roles.

What normal roles? he asked himself.

Sabrina was the brand new dance teacher at the cultural arts middle school where he taught jazz history and band. That was when it all had started, he realized, coming to the understanding that what he really needed to do was find a way to deal with her without hurting her feelings. He always hated hurting her feelings. John had nicknamed her Pest because that was what she had always been to him and his twin brother Josh. They couldn't be within twenty feet of their sister's house without Sabrina pestering them about something. While Josh would shoo her away with hash words, John had always found himself saying something to soothe the sting. Once, he had even given her his last five dollars when she was selling candy for school because Josh had been so rude to her.

Sabrina stirred again, interrupting his thoughts. This time her eyes blinked open. A slow smile spread across her full lips as she tilted her head toward him. Don't say a word, his eyes pleaded, hoping that she wouldn't comment on his current state.

"Nice view," she told him, sitting up and easing into a wide stretch, his shirt dropping to her lap. The stretchy cotton material of her tank top pulled across her breasts, which he refused to look at, staring into her eyes instead, which wasn't much better. She had some sexy eyes.

Deep brown.

Inquisitive.

Knowing.

Knowing?

What exactly could she know?

What exactly did she know?

"What are you thinking?" he asked, not realizing that he had posed his question aloud.

"I was thinking that I should thank you. I knew I could count on you."

"For what?" he asked, losing his train of thought, sinking into her brown eyes. *Count on me to lose control, wanting someone I have no business wanting?*

"For making it up to me."

John blinked in an effort to shake himself free of whatever her eyes were doing to him so that he could follow the conversation. "What are you talking about?" he finally asked.

"You were extremely rude to me last night, but I forgive you because you made it up to me."

"How?"

"By being my human pillow and by not letting me freeze. I was cold last night, but it's hot now. Do you want your shirt back?"

At his nod Sabrina handed him the shirt. A soft smile remained on her face, along with that knowing look making him extremely uncomfortable.

"It *is* hot," John told her, not knowing what else to say. He had figured the heat he had been feeling had everything to do with her, but now he realized that it was more than that.

"I think the power's out," Sabrina leaned toward him to say, a hand on each thigh.

"Stop it, Pest," he told her, using the old pet name to put their relationship back into perspective.

"Only when you stop."

"I'm not doing anything."

"Exactly."

"And that's how it's going to be. There can't anything between us. I have no time for a relationship."

"That's what you said the other night. I get it." She leaned into him. Sabrina couldn't help herself. He was so warm and handsome and she was remembering the kiss she had stolen. Well, not exactly stolen. Initiated would be the correct word. She had started it but John had certainly gotten plenty involved before he ended it. As she leaned closer, John leaned back, his head tapping the seat of the bleacher behind him, but Sabrina didn't let that stop her. The warmth of the room, the heat between them, the slashing rain and wind did nothing to make her pause. If anything, it pulled them together. Though the room was filled with a few hundred people, Sabrina felt as if it was theirs alone and they were taking up where they had left off. Her lips a mere breath away, Sabrina felt his hands on her wrists.

"Sabrina, no."

"Yes," she breathed across his lips, forgetting the rejection, wanting only to feel the heat of his lips and the thrill of being in his arms. Sabrina had known that no kiss would compare to John's. And she was right because she had kissed quite a few guys, all experiments, the experiences saved for future reference. Well, most recent reference, but never anything more.

"Stop acting like a child," he was saying, his hands giving her wrist a squeeze before he stood and climbed to a higher row.

Sabrina looked up at him, surprised at her own actions as well as his reaction. She didn't run after guys. That wasn't her style. Beyond her kissing experiments, she didn't have much use for just any old guy. She had long ago recognized that John was her man and it was time that she claimed him. "I can't believe you're running away from me, but I know why," she whispered up to him, not wanting to wake every soul in the shelter.

"Right, sure you do, Pest."

It was the use of that old nickname that made her say what she said next. "Right is right. You're running because you're scared. You care about me and I turn you on just as much as you turn me on and you can't deal with that."

He had jumped down from his safety perch before she had time to process that he was standing in front of her again. "What I care about, Pest, is my music, and I'm mature enough to know that this *turn on* can be turned off. I'm not interested. Try playing these games with your trooper friend."

As soon as the words left his lips, John was sorry he had uttered them. Lowered lids and a downward twist of her mouth now shuttered the excitement, passion and confidence he had seen in her eyes.

"Ma'am, sir, I'm going to have to ask you to come down," a voice intruded before John could apologize.

"Speak of the devil," he muttered as Sabrina turned toward the voice of the man leaning over the rail.

"Yes?" she softly asked.

"Come down, please."

"Certainly, Officer," she answered.

The voice turned hard. "Both you and the gentleman."

"Of course," John answered, handing Sabrina his shirt. "Put this on."

"Why?"

"That thing you're wearing is too—"

"Too insignificant to you. You shouldn't care. After all, your music is what you care about."

She was on the gym floor and in deep conversation with the state trooper by the time he had collected his backpack and trumpet and made his way down, knowing that he had made the right decision in the worst possible way.

CHAPTER 3

Bent on making John jealous, Sabrina followed the trooper, who motioned her away from the slowly waking crowd.

"Is there a problem, ma'am?" he asked, a sincere look of concern on his face.

"No," Sabrina told him, knowing there was no way that she could flirt with this sweet man without feeling guilty. Besides, she wasn't good at it. Peering over her shoulder, she saw John struggling to make his way down from the bleachers with his precious trumpet in hand. Just because she couldn't do it, didn't mean John couldn't *think* she was flirting.

"Are you sure?"

"Absolutely. If you don't mind me asking, why are you still here?"

"When I tried the leave, the wind and rain had worsened. I couldn't make it back to the station so I reported in and came back here instead."

"Oh," Sabrina said, her attention drawn by a loud thump.

"What was that?" A voice that sounded like the loud man from the van echoed through the room, waking most of the other people in the shelter.

"He's pretty clumsy," the trooper commented.

"Not normally."

"So you know that man?"

"Yes, he's an *old* family friend," Sabrina said just as John walked up.

"How can I help you, officer?" John asked when he finally made it over to them.

"You can help by cooling down. You made enough noise to wake everyone and the tension between you two had me about ready to drag somebody off to jail despite the storm. But since the lady here has no complaint—"

"Is there a problem here, Trooper Dan?" the director of the shelter, the same woman who'd announced lights out a few hours ago, asked.

"No, Mrs. Broussard," the trooper said.

"No, none whatsoever," Sabrina answered a mere two seconds later.

"None whatsoever," John echoed.

"Do you have any news on the storm?" The woman directed her question to the trooper.

The inquiry focused Sabrina on the situation at hand. John had caused her mind to drift away from their current circumstance. Although she was sure that they would be back home in a matter of days, she still had to get through it, contact her grandmother and uncle, and have her car repaired so that she could get to them.

"The storm made landfall about an hour ago."

"But wasn't it supposed to hit in the morning?" John asked the trooper, who threw him a hard stare in response.

"Yes, wasn't it?" Sabrina asked.

The trooper smiled at her and went on, "It is morning."

"But it's so dark."

"The power is out in all of southeast Louisiana, Ms.—."

"Sabrina," she supplied, much too readily, John thought.

"Exactly where are we?" John asked, realizing that he lost track of his location when he had run out of gas. This time the trooper looked at him with disgust.

"Kentwood, Louisiana." He paused before adding, "sir."

If John wasn't already sure that he had been painted the bad guy, the man's attitude confirmed it. He decided to keep his mouth shut. Sabrina was getting him into trouble that went beyond the personal kind.

"The home of Brittney Spears," Sabrina said.

"That it is." The muscular man smiled, towering over Sabrina.

John frowned, knowing that the trooper just looked bigger because of the police vest he wore. The thing made his brother Randy, who worked for the New Orleans Police Department, look bigger than he actually was, too. Then there was all the equipment hanging from his waist, adding to the man's dimensions. John gritted his teeth, something he had never done before, which was amazing, since he was the youngest in a large family, had a twin and a crew of brothers and sisters, in-laws, nieces and nephews he called family.

"The storm?" the shelter director asked again.

"It's still raging outside. We're still experiencing squalls and will be for some time."

"Any news from New Orleans?"

He paused just a fraction of a second before answering, "Nothing conclusive."

"Okay then, keep us informed. I better get breakfast started."

"Can I help?" Sabrina asked the other woman, needing to get away from both the trooper and John. She had not meant to, but had somehow gained a protector she wasn't sure she wanted.

"Yes, thank you. My name's Kathy Broussard. We're short handed . . ." The woman's voice trailed away.

"I'll just find my way to the restroom before the crowd—" John began.

"We're not finished talking," the other man said. John knew the trooper was younger than his own twenty-eight years. He had a fresh rookie look about him.

John kept a steady pleasant expression as the trooper went on. He was used to keeping his cool. It was his twin who had always been the hothead. John soon realized that his ploy didn't seem to be working. The trooper went on and on, leaving no doubt in John's mind that if it were up to the trooper he would be in jail.

"You won't get any trouble out me, officer," John said once the trooper had wound down.

"See that I don't." He walked off in the same direction Sabrina had taken a few minutes ago. John wisely headed in the other direction, thinking, "My mama didn't raise no fool." And if Sabrina was interested in the man, then that at least would keep her out of his hair. Which was exactly where he wanted her.

Yeah, exactly where he wanted her.

The few minutes it took him to get back to the gym had been all the time needed for the area to became a beehive of activity. People of all shapes and sizes, ages and races moved about. Soon Kathy Broussard appeared, gaining everyone's attention with the ringing of an old fashioned hand bell. After a short speech welcoming everyone, she asked latecomers to sign in and went through a list of rules and procedures that no one seemed to have a problem following.

"Remember, we're all in this together. In a few hours we will have ridden out the storm and in a day or two you will all be able to return home. In the meantime, make some new friends."

Considering the fact that they were stuck indoors with a storm raging outside, the wind and rain slashing across the high windows of the gym, what else could they do? What else would Sabrina do? he asked himself as he watched her.

All day John found himself watching her.

She and the trooper placed portable camp lamps at various places around the gym. John offered his services to Kathy, who directed him to the cafeteria, where he carried crates of milk and yogurt to a serving table, while watching Sabrina place more lamps in the cafeteria with the help of Trooper Dan.

"We have to give out these dairy products before they go bad. We have only minimal ice."

"Sure," John answered, watching Sabrina talking to a little girl who was smiling up at her.

Soon the cafeteria was filled with people ready for a morning meal. John placed himself at the far end of the line passing out cereal while Sabrina, Trooper Dan, and Kathy worked at the other end. Even so, John found himself watching her as she smiled, made funny faces for the kids, and cracked corny jokes. She made him feel good inside. Too good, he decided, vowing to stay even farther away from her.

Finding his way to a table at the opposite side of the room from where she sat with Trooper Dan, John took in the talk at various tables. Evacuation stories dominated the conversations. The stories were all different but somehow the same, and all tinged with an anxiousness to get back home and a hope that the wind and floodwaters didn't do too much damage.

"We'll be home the day after tomorrow. Just wait and see," a large man said. Everyone at the table nodded in agreement.

Someone dared to disagree with the big man. "I don't know, this one looks bad."

"Betsy in '65 was bad, but the city survived."

Nobody could deny that fact, so no one did.

Feeling restless, John decided to make himself scarce. A small corner mid-way up the bleachers became his sanctuary. He sat quietly, refusing to even think about the reason he needed a sanctuary. He was used to noise. He had lived with it all of his life. Sabrina liked it, too. She seemed to thrive under the constant bustle of a large family and loved being around his.

That was it!

This explained her behavior.

Sabrina was transferring the love she felt for his family to him because of the whole hurricane evacuation thing. This attraction was just misplaced desire to feel loved and safe and secure. What she really desired was being around his family. *Then why did she come on to you at the casino when there wasn't even a hint of worry about the hurricane coming their way?* a voice inside his head asked. Well, he had no answer for that one but knew Sabrina loved being around his family. Maybe she was going after him to become a permanent part of the Lewis clan. John blew out a breath as he blew that thought away as ridiculous. He got more comfortable on his perch of solitude and continued to watch Sabrina.

He couldn't help himself.

In the course of the morning she must have talked to at least fifty different people. She held a fussy baby for an exhausted young mother and played cards with an old man. Near lunchtime, he watched as she gathered a group of antsy kids for an impromptu dance lesson. The sight prompted him to do more than watch. Taking out his trumpet he made his way across the bleachers and stopped just above the area she had cleared. He began to play a lively jazz tune. She stopped in the middle of a turn she had been demonstrating and smiled up at him. That smile squeezed his heart, wildly distributing warmth and pleasure deep inside of him. She danced in a follow-the-leader sort of way as he played, the children giggling and burning all their pent-up energy as they followed along. Parents and adults stopped to listen. The entire gym was filled with the sound of laughter and music.

"One of the levees broke!" someone yelled, shattering the joy of the moment.

"What?"

"Which levee?"

"Where'd you hear that?"

"My radio, I finally got it working. They said the city's flooded. There's water everywhere!"

"Everywhere?"

"What do you mean by everywhere?"

"I don't know, everywhere!"

"And the Superdome's damaged."

"The Superdome!"

A rising murmur escalated into a loud buzz of anxiousness and fear. Trooper Dan and Kathy were attempting to calm the crowd, but the growing fear and a need for answers drowned out their attempts. The kids, reacting to the tension in the air, surrounded Sabrina, who looked up at him. Her look seemed to say, "You can do something about this." The only something he could think of was to play. Music was known to soothe and the rising tempest in the shelter needed to be calmed. John let out a bugle call, then eased into a slow jazzy tune far different from the lively one he had played for the kids. He played until he felt the tension lessen. When he looked down into the crowd Kathy had the unused bell in her hand, Trooper Dan was walking up toward him, and Sabrina was sitting in the midst of the children. Everyone's attention was centered on him.

"Whatever this hurricane has done to our city, we'll handle it," John told the crowd.

Several heads nodded in agreement.

"Thanks," Trooper Dan said, a respect in his eye John had not seen before.

As the trooper spoke, the crowd threw questions at him that he obviously had no answer to. The discussion ended with Trooper Dan promising to get more information after lunch was served.

A more subdued crowd entered the cafeteria. The windows were open now that the rain had stopped. The quiet in the room was broken only by the static coming from the radio and the sporadic cries of an infant. No one wanted to believe what they'd heard. The entire city could not be flooded.

After helping to serve a lunch of sandwich crackers, fruit, milk and juice, John sought Sabrina out. They ate in silence. Simply being near each other seemed to ease the frustration of the unknown. His mom, a wise woman, had always told him to worry only when he had to. And right now he didn't have all the facts. Thankfully his entire family was out of harm's way and he was relatively safe. Then suddenly he remembered.

"Randy!"

"What about Randy?" Sabrina asked.

"He's a cop. He had to stay in the city. If it's flooded . . . Sabrina, he could be injured or–"

"No, don't say that. Randy is fine. He's smart and knows how to take care of himself."

"You're right. He's been a cop for over ten years. He's fine." John's hand tapped the table as he looked around.

"Your trumpet's on the floor next to you."

"I know."

"Do you need to play it?"

"No, I need to find out if my brother's okay. I need a radio that works, a television, a phone that I can get through on. I need a landline. Something."

Just then Sabrina's cell phone gave a strange ring. Pulling the phone out of her pocket, she flipped it open. "It's a text message, John. I hadn't thought about it. We can't call but maybe we can text." If so, she could have texted her uncle a long time ago. The message read: "Where r u?"

As she sent an answer to her message, John was digging into his pocket and seconds later sending a message of his own. Soon the others caught on and contacted loved ones and received more information about what was happening in the city.

"He's okay. He's trapped in a hospital in New Orleans East. He's hot, bothered, and stuck. The East is flooded," John told her.

The cafeteria filled with more news of flooding, loved ones slowly creating a picture of devastation that Sabrina was finding hard to believe. Just twenty-four hours ago her only worries had been a bad radiator and getting John to notice her.

He looked at her, reached a hand over and claimed one of hers.

For the rest of the day as news trickled in about the rising flood waters and multiple leeve breaks, John was at her side.

Once again they helped to serve dinner that consisted of the same fare they'd had for lunch, due to a delay in supplies reaching the shelter.

That night, without saying a word to each other, they went up into the bleachers together. Sabrina settled between his legs, with no thought of stealing a kiss or declaring her love.

"John, I can't even imagine what I'm hearing. The entire Ninth Ward, most of New Orleans East, and Lakeview all under water?"

"My mind can't picture it either."

"Then we won't. Put your arms around me and make me feel better."

"Sure, 'Brina. I can do that."

"Much better."

"What?"

"I like 'Brina a whole lot better than Pest."

"I know."

"I feel better already. I knew I could count on you. That's why I love you, John," she sighed.

John held his tongue, knowing that this wasn't the time to remind Sabrina that there couldn't be anything between them. What she needed was some comfort and reassurance that all was not lost. She needed it just as much as he did.

CHAPTER 4

Surreal.

For the first time in her life Sabrina was truly experiencing the meaning of that word. None of what was happening felt as if it was real, as if it was happening—

—*in* her life.

—*in* her city.

—*to* her community.

But the pictures flashing across the screen in all their seven-inch glory were actually real.

Huddled next to John, her eyes glued to the screen, Sabrina felt an overabundance of emotion tighten her stomach and race up her spine to lodge in her heart.

Her city was flooded.

Not just flooded, it was drowning in devastation and there didn't seem to be a life preserver within reach.

New Orleans was drowning and people were suffering. Its people were the heart of the city and Sabrina watched as the city's pulse became more and more erratic.

She couldn't tear her eyes away from the miniature screen as one horrific scene after another flashed before her eyes.

There were people walking through water.

Trapped on rooftops.

On rooftops!

In the middle of summer.

Summer in New Orleans was a sweltering, humid steam bath. Any one of the hundreds waiting for rescue would gladly trade places with her. A number of times today Sabrina had wished whole families, the old and sick, could magically take the place of the loud-mouth complainer who griped about the lack of air conditioning in the powerless, but safe, shelter they were lucky enough to occupy.

An empathetic moan rose from the pit of her stomach as the scene changed to show a man pushing a pool raft holding a small, wiggling bundle toward higher ground. The man slipped, his head sinking into the polluted flood waters. John lifted an arm to pull her closer, instantly sticking to her perspiration-wet shoulder.

"John, Sabrina," Kathy Broussard called, bringing with her a sliver of light from the foyer. "I know I said that you could watch the news after lights out but you've been in here for hours." She stood in front of the portable television completely blocking the small screen since neither of them seemed to have fully registered her presence. "This isn't good. Not only are you going to run down my batteries, but you'll run yourself to the ground staring at this kind of misery for hours on end."

"But Kathy, you don't understand—" Sabrina started.

"It's our city, our community, and those people stuck there could have been us," John finished on a strange gruff note, his eyes stretched wide.

"I do understand, which is why, right now, you're going to move away from this."

"That's impossible. It doesn't matter if you turn it off or not. I can still see it all!" Sabrina stood with John following suit, his expression reflecting her words.

"—and digest what you've seen," Kathy continued as if she hadn't been interrupted, "and decide where to go from there." As she finished she laid a hand on each of their shoulders.

Sabrina looked to John, who gave a slight nod of agreement, repeating the movement in Kathy's direction. Kathy had no problem interpreting the nod. "Good. Besides, a huge truck just pulled up. It's the supplies we've been waiting for from the Red Cross."

"The supplies we've been waiting for?" Sabrina asked, confused for a moment.

"Food, cots, blankets, a couple of volunteers and hopefully a generator or two."

Sabrina's spirits lifted. "That's great. If we're getting supplies here, then the Red Cross, Coast Guard and every other agency has to be doing even more for all those people stuck in New Orleans."

"I'm sure they must be," Kathy agreed.

"I'll text Randy to see what he knows."

"But he hasn't answered any of your text messages since yesterday morning."

"He's saving the battery power on his cell phone, 'Brina. There's no electricity and Randy doesn't have access to a car to charge his phone."

"Then we're lucky to have Trooper Dan helping us out."

Dan had offered to charge their cell phone in his car so that they could continue to have contact with family members now that they had discovered that text messages would go through. John appreciated the trooper's help more than he'd ever know. Being able to contact his older brother at least once a day to know that he was still alive and "hanging in there" helped John to keep his head. Not to mention the boost he got from daily updates from other members of his family.

"John? What were you saying about Randy?"

Focusing on Sabrina, he was relieved to see the deep sadness surrounding her had lifted a degree or two since she'd shifted her attention from the events happening in the city. Kathy was right, they both needed to step away from the misery, for a little while at least. "Just that Randy's going to contact me around seven," he finally answered.

"What time is it now?"

"Six in the a.m.," Kathy answered. "How about we help those volunteers unload the cots and supplies."

Sabrina pushed the disturbing images to the back of her mind and set herself to doing what she could for the people that she *could* help. With John at her side she could get through this. Instead of wallowing in self-pity she decided to count her blessings as she followed Kathy and John.

Thanks to text technology, her grandmother and Uncle Darren knew that she was safe.

John was with her.

She was alive and well.

John was with her.

" 'Brina, grab the other end of this stack," he called to her, using the name she loved. It rumbled past his lips with a possessiveness he probably had no idea existed.

"Sure," she answered, an inner smile lifting her spirits. She kept herself occupied the remainder of the day with helping to unload, prepare *hot* meals, distribute supplies and help a few of her special friends who needed a bit of extra help getting settled in. The old man and his son, Mr. Raymond and Ray, Jr., had some issues with opening the cots. The young single mother didn't have enough hands to even consider attempting to do so on her own. Sabrina occupied her own hands and mind for as long as she could, hoping that those still stuck in the city were receiving similar aid.

Making her way up to what had become her usual spot in the bleachers, Sabrina paused to take a deep breath. She surveyed the huge gym, appreciating the coolness of the air thanks to the generators brought in by the Red Cross volunteers as well as the difference in the atmosphere. The despondency that had hung in the air had been transformed into hope because a few basic needs had been met.

Food and a comfortable place to sleep were things usually taken for granted but deeply appreciated now.

The lights flickered. "Lights out in fifteen minutes," Kathy Broussard announced.

Scanning the gym floor for John, Sabrina spotted him coming out of the little back room where Kathy secretly kept the portable television they had watched for hours on end the night before. He stopped to talk to Trooper Dan, who had just come in. It was strange how they had become such good friends over the past two days. "Guys," Sabrina thought as she shrugged her shoulders. The jealously thing hadn't been working too well anyway. Not that anything else had been. Not that she had time to try anything else. Too much had been happening. The world as they knew it had completely changed with the violent winds and rain of Hurricane Katrina. Sabrina's whole being had been too concentrated on her grandmother, the hurricane and the effects of it all to focus on her situation with John, though she felt as if they were moving toward . . .

Toward something.

Which was more than the nothing he wanted.

The lights flashed again. "Five minutes," Kathy announced.

Sabrina watched the intensity of the conversation between John and Trooper Dan increase, reading John's body language enough to know that he was upset about something.

"Are we getting a lullaby tonight?" someone called from the gym floor.

"Where's our trumpet player?" someone else asked.

"John, they're calling for you." Kathy's voice rang out across the now quiet gym.

Holding up his trumpet case, Sabrina silently invited him up. She could see that the last thing he wanted to do was end his conversation, but he did, knowing how important his music had become to the people staying with them in the shelter.

Bounding up the stairs, he paused to stare into her eyes. Worry and deep anxiety were plainly there before he looked down into the case she held open. Trumpet in hand, his eyes met hers once again, the light of love nearly blinding her before he placed the instrument to his lips. Sabrina took a step back and lowered herself to the bleachers as a sweet sound burst from the brass instrument under the loving caress of John's fingers. As the melody of the song "Do You Know What it Means", made famous by Louis Armstrong, flowed out into the gym, Sabrina suddenly wondered for the first time how she could possibly compete with his love for music. As the last note floated away into the silent gym it was obvious that everyone was reflecting in their own way exactly how much each and every one of them was missing New Orleans.

The lights went out and the only sound was the soft rustle and creak of people settling onto their respective cots. Her eyes still adjusting to the change in lighting, Sabrina heard more than saw the loving way John handled the instrument.

Suddenly she was tired.

Too tired to attempt to compete with John's love of music.

Too tired to ask about his conversation with Trooper Dan.

Even too tired to worry about it.

When John settled himself on the bleacher behind her, she rested her head against his leg, her tired body leading her brain into slumber.

For her.

He was playing a song for her in a small, dimly lit room. *A room with a bed.* The song, a jazzy tune that vibrated between them, was seeping under her skin and sending the message that he cared. The music he made was definite proof that it was possible to combine his love for her with his love for music. A shiny gold band shone brightly on his left hand; a matching one glistened on *her* left.

"Our honeymoon," Sabrina thought.

At the end of the song John tossed the trumpet to the side, pulling her into his arms and stroking her with such reverence and intensity that Sabrina felt tears well in her eyes from the beauty of it all. But somehow, in the midst of this wonderful dream, a thought burrowed its way into her consciousness.

Something was seriously wrong.

Something she should have addressed.

Sabrina's eyes jerked opened with that persistent thought. She almost groaned aloud when she realized that John was no longer cradling her face between his hands. That was one thing that was absolutely wrong, but not what had awakened her with such nagging insistence.

It was because of John talking to Trooper Dan right after he came out of the back room, the back room with the television. Something more had happened. Something he wasn't telling her. What could possibly be worse than the scenes she had already viewed for hours last night? Sabrina had no idea but the thought had taken hold and wouldn't let go.

Something *was* seriously wrong.

She would to go see for herself. Carefully, she lifted her head, paused a second to see if the movement would wake him, then scooted down to the next row of bleachers.

"Where are you going, 'Brina?"

"The bathroom," she automatically replied, not wanting him to know that she suspected that he was keeping something from her. She stood, realizing that she really did have to go, which absolved her from the little white lie she had told.

"Be careful," he muttered, repositioning himself and pulling his backpack closer to use as a pillow.

"Sure," she agreed, easily making her way down to the floor, making a quick stop in the bathroom. Her reflection in the mirror reminded her that she was still wearing John's shirt. He had let her borrow it after taking a shower for the first time in the last three days. She still didn't have a change of clothes since her suitcase was inside her car and the supplies delivered today had nothing to do with clothing. The shirt was comfortable, like John himself. At least like the John of her dreams who she had been about to feel draped all over her if it hadn't been for the worry that had lodged in her head.

Turning the television on, Sabrina settled herself onto the floor. Her suspicions were confirmed when the same news channel they had been watching appeared on the screen. Focused on what the reporter was saying, Sabrina didn't hear the door open.

"What are you doing?" John demanded. "I thought you were going to the bathroom," he accused, giving her no time to answer.

"I was. And now I'm here trying to figure out what the news about the city that you're trying to keep from me."

"What are you talking about?"

"Don't 'what are you talking about' me, John Lewis. I've known you long enough to tell when you're keeping a secret."

"How?" he asked, turning the television off, then reaching down to cradle her elbows and pull her to her feet. The warmth of his hands worked its way up her arms, then spread like wildfire to heat her entire body.

"What do you mean, how?"

John had expected to find her sitting in front of the television, and that he would have to convince her to walk away from the mesmerizing screen. A bit of teasing could do the trick. Besides, he'd always liked to tease her. Of course that was before he became aware of her as a woman. But maybe a bit of lighthearted teasing could help him ease her back into the kid category again. "Give me an example of when you've noticed that I've had a secret."

"What difference does it make?"

"Then you don't have any examples. Which means that you don't know me as well as you think you do."

"Of course I do."

"Then prove it."

"I knew that you knew about Ness and Scott going out long before anyone else."

"Of course you knew. Josh knew, too. We were all there that day when Scott showed up at Ness's house, remember?"

"But you were the only one who knew it was serious. That it would lead to love and marriage."

"Maybe," he said, remembering that was exactly what he had thought when he'd seen Ness and Scott together for the first time. "What else do you have?" he demanded, his fingers massaging her elbows, moving a bit higher with a soft gentle caress.

"Monica and Devin."

"What about my oldest sister and her husband?" John asked, his hand suddenly itching to explore more of the softness beneath his fingers.

"You knew they were going to get married. Everyone else thought they were friends, but you weren't surprised when they all of a sudden decided to get married."

"So that's what you think?"

"That's what I know."

"So you do know me better than I thought."

"You had better believe it."

"Then you realize that against my better judgment I'm about to kiss you."

"I knew that from the minute you touched me. I felt it in your hands, in the way your fingers—" Sabrina paused. The look, the intense expression he wore, was the exact one she had seen earlier as he played his trumpet.

"The way my fingers ached to touch you? Was that what you were going to say, 'Brina?"

"No, but I'm relieved to hear you say it because my body itches to be touched, but . . ."

"But?"

"But only by you."

"Then we'll have to do something about that," John heard himself say. There was no way he could push 'Brina back into the kid category ever again. She was all *woman,* and he wanted her. There was nothing he could do to stop the wanting that was as vital a need to his system as his music had always been. His fingers moved up into the short sleeves of the shirt. Cupping her shoulders, he pulled her toward him.

Memory of the wild kiss they had shared in Mississippi, backstage, in a tight dark corner, sparked into a passionate eagerness he could barely contain. Yet, when his lips lay against hers, instead of wildly claiming her lips, John slowly drew from hers a sensual magic that sent a flood of blood to his groin. Then a soft murmur from her lips caused all manner of passion to break loose.

His kiss stirred a sweetness, restlessness and frustration all at once. It filled her heart with an affirmation of his feelings for her. No man kissed a woman the way he was kissing her unless she meant something to him. Sweet as the kiss was, remnants of her dream left Sabrina wanting so much more. Without breaking the spell, she made a sound, a kind of questioning moan, to communicate what she wanted. A second later John was exactly where she wanted him.

All over her.

More accurately, she was all over him.

Somehow John had lowered them to the floor, his arms still inside the sleeves of the shirt she was wearing, his hands a heated presence pulling her flush against him. His lips tugged and pulled from her a passion she saved for him alone.

"I need to touch you," he said on a harsh breath.

"You are touching me," Sabrina breathed into his mouth.

"Not where and definitely not how I want to."

His hands slid off her shoulders, leaving a scorching trail of heat as they traveled down her arms. A ripping sound caused him to pause.

"Shirt got stuck on my watch," he explained. "I don't care," John muttered between heated nips at her chin, her neck and her collarbone. He couldn't get enough of her. To caress and stroke every part of her had became his sole goal. He wanted to make her sing. Rolling so that she was beneath him, he had every intention of doing just that. Here, at this moment, holding back made absolutely no sense. His world right now made no sense. He had no home, no job. Nothing was certain except the fact Sabrina was offering herself to him and he wanted her. He wanted to be in her comforting arms. He wanted to comfort her. For a few minutes he didn't want to think about devastation and lives lost. He didn't want to think about his brother stranded in the hellhole New Orleans had become.

Pressing his lower body into hers, he froze. A vibration shimmered down his thigh. It took a second for him to realize that it wasn't part of his intense reaction to Sabrina.

"My phone!" he yelled.

"Your phone," Sabrina said, icy disappointment in her tone.

"It has to be Randy. I didn't hear from him at all yesterday."

He took a long calming breath, and in a soft, deep voice began telling her all the news he had been holding back. "There are terrible things happening in the city. People are looting stores and houses for food and water, which makes sense to me right now, but some are just outright stealing. Police are getting shot at."

At his explanation Sabrina scooted over to him, pressing her body against his back, she wrapped her arms around him.

As he fumbled in his pocket for his phone, he turned to face her, his eyes boring into hers. "One cop, shot himself. He couldn't take the pressure, so— he— *shot*— himself." John turned away from her, as he finally pulled the phone out of his pocket.

Leaning forward, Sabrina took the phone from his shaking hands. "Randy wouldn't do that. He couldn't do that. He knows he has a huge family counting on him to stay alive. When I open this phone you'll see the proof for yourself."

Opening the text box Sabrina read,

still alive

2 busy 2 text
saved by cops with a boat
saved others
floated by my house
its a lake
new station on chef
not flooded
no worries
luv

"Did you understand all that?" Sabrina asked.

"Every word. Randy's finally been rescued by fellow police officers from the hospital in New Orleans East. He probably saw his house filled to the roof. And it sounds like they've set up a new station somewhere on Chef Highway, which miraculously hasn't flooded. He doesn't want us to worry and—"

Sabrina waited.

"And he says that he loves us." A huge breath caused his shoulders to expand, pressing into her chest. The brief contact sent a heated reminder of the passion they'd just shared. Interrupted but not forgotten. "I know he loves us, we're family, but I can't remember Randy—*ever.* I mean—I know he does. But he's one of my older brothers and a cop and all. Those aren't words he says."

"These are special circumstances. I think that now is a good time to share those kinds of feelings."

"You're right."

Arms still around him, Sabrina closed the phone. "Now would also be a good time to continue where we left off," she said, placing a feather light kiss on his neck.

John jerked away, was on his feet and halfway to the door before Sabrina digested that he was running away from her again.

"What we started in here wasn't a good idea, Sabrina," he said as he stood at the door, the knob in his hand. "I was worried about Randy, my family and the state of our city. I stand by what I told you in Mississippi," he finished before walking through the door.

Moving almost as quickly as he had, Sabrina was only a moment or two behind him. "Don't run away from me!" she told his retreating back.

"I'm not running. I'm going for a walk to cool off."

"And exactly why is it so necessary to cool off?" Sabrina demanded, darting in front of him, determined to make it as difficult as possible for him to run away from her, from them.

"Because I'm not about to take advantage of you during this stressful time in your life."

"That's a crock of—"

"Sabrina, is that you?" Looking to the opposite end of the hall, she saw old Mr. Raymond standing with a confused expression on his face. "Can you give an old man a hand?" he asked, shuffling toward her.

"Sure thing, Mr. Raymond," Sabrina answered, glancing back in time to see John make good his escape. As he dashed out the door to the outside she got a quick look at the rising sun, giving her a clue as to what time it was. Soon the entire shelter would be roused and ready for breakfast. He wasn't going to get away that easily.

She'd catch up with him before the usual duties of the day occupied them both.

"I got up to use the bathroom and looks like I've got myself all mixed up," her old friend explained as she met him halfway.

"Anybody could get a little mixed up." Sabrina smiled up at him, attempting to keep her frustration with John off her face. It wasn't Mr. Raymond's fault that John was a coward.

"That's me, Mixed-up Raymond," he chuckled at himself.

Sabrina laughed with him as she guided him back toward the gym, helping him to maneuver his way back to his assigned area.

"I didn't want to wake Ray. Thanks for being my angel of mercy." He smiled up at her, making her glad she had taken the time to help.

"Where have you been, Dad?" Sabrina heard Ray ask his father just as they made it to their little corner of the gym.

"On a lovely stroll with a beautiful young woman," he answered, winking at her.

Sabrina smiled once again and dashed off because, sure enough, the gym was coming to life.

"Sabrina! Can you—" Kathy called out to her as Sabrina reached the front door.

Not giving Kathy a chance to say what she needed her to do, Sabrina called, "I'll be back in a minute," and pulled the front door closed behind her.

Walking the perimeter of the school without finding any sign of John, she was about to give up when she spotted a small building behind the school. Without hesitation she dashed toward it, certain that she'd find him there.

"Can't you leave well enough alone, Pest?" were the words that greeted her.

She hadn't expected open arms or a kiss but the sting of the words and the use of the offensive nickname was still a surprise, almost enough to make her turn back but she was not a coward. She knew what she wanted and she knew what she felt for him even if he didn't.

"All I want is to have an adult conversation with you. I'm an adult now, John, not a little kid with a crush on you."

"You're not a kid. I understand that much," John told her, his eyes taking in what lay beneath his unbuttoned shirt. "But you're still way too young for me and you're doing nothing more than elevating a crush to a physical level." Recognizing the determined look on her face, he searched his mind for something that would cut the conversation and end her pursuit. Too bad Josh wasn't here to whisper a little something in his ear.

"John—"

He cut her off with the first thing that came to mind. "And I'm not about to rob the cradle."

"Rob the cradle! I'm not a little teeny-bopper any more. You're only seven years older."

"Seven years more mature, seven years more experienced." He walked away, having obviously hit the mark because she stood stunned, speechless, for at least ten seconds before following him. John headed back toward the school with hopes of avoiding any further discussion by surrounding himself with people. He needed to make plans beyond this day-to-day existence in a shelter.

Catching up to him just before he got to the door, Sabrina reached for him. Desperate for him to simply take her seriously, she pulled at his arm, forcing him to face her. "John Lewis—" She paused, not knowing what to say. Outside noises filtered into her subconscious. The sounds of birds, a car coming up the graveled path, John's rapid breathing, or maybe it was hers. Suddenly she *felt* inexperienced, immature and completely insecure.

He looked down at her hand and then into her eyes with his own eyes still saying he wanted her. "What do you want, 'Brina?"

"You," she whispered, falling back on the only thing she was certain of, the physical attraction between them. Reaching up to him, she wrapped her arms around his neck, pressed herself against his hard body and kissed lips that, at first, wouldn't accept her. But only for a moment or two. His mouth opened beneath hers and—

"Sabrina Adams, what the hell are you doing!" A thoroughly disgusted, loud, angry voice interrupted her progress.

"Uncle Darren," Sabrina squeaked, turning to find said relative standing a few feet away.

"Have you lost your mind?"

Feeling every inch the teeny-booper she had denied being and figuring that the question was rhetorical, Sabrina stood up straighter and simply waited.

"Well?" her uncle asked, correcting her impression of the type of question he had asked. Finding it difficult to answer without affirming John's opinion of her and making herself look like a fool, Sabrina was at a loss as to how to react. How would a mature, experienced person react in a situation where an uncle, who was more like a father, caught her throwing herself at a man?

"You were raised better than this. I saw the whole thing. Why were you chasing that man and pressing yourself against him?"

"He's not just any man. It's John, Uncle Darren." Sabrina stepped away, knowing that a mature, experienced person probably would not have pointed that out.

"Which doesn't make the situation any better. I oughta take you back home and lock you up myself." He directed this last statement at John in a quiet, deadly voice.

"Darren, I—" John paused but continued a minute later. "Guilty as charged. You can lock me up and throw away the key."

"Don't think I won't."

"I'm pretty certain you would. Just know that this won't ever, *ever,*" he emphasized, directing his gaze her way, "happen again."

Staring at John for a good long while, Darren finally answered, "I'll take your word for it. And you," his bushy eyebrows slanted downward, "have you no self respect? What would Grammy think if she saw you? She'd have another anxiety attack."

Sabrina was in the act of drawing enough courage to maturely, though respectfully, inform her uncle that she was all grown up and that it was her business to whom she chose to give her attention as well as the when and where, when his words sank in.

"What's wrong with Grammy?"

"Worry is what's wrong with Grammy." He rubbed a hand down his face, which immediately transformed into a weary mask. "When I got home from work late last night, she was so worked up she could barely breathe. It got so bad I had to rush her to the hospital."

"Her heart?" Sabrina's own skipped a beat, guilt finding its way inside as she listened to her grandmother's youngest son.

"As strong as can be expected. Her body's just reacting to everything that's happened. Having you missing and then so far away made it all worse."

"The text message I sent didn't ease her mind?"

"She wanted you there in front of her in body, not spirit."

"I was going to come, just as soon as I got my car fixed. Trooper Dan was going to help me."

"Another man? Tell him not to bother, it's being towed to Lafayette right now."

So much had happened. Her grandmother should not have had to go through more trauma. It was all because of her. If she hadn't been chasing after John in Mississippi, and again here, she could have saved Grammy some grief. And it was all for nothing. Sabrina felt like a fool.

"As soon as she was discharged she made me come out to find you," her uncle was saying. "I've found you. Get your things. Let's go."

"There's nothing here for me," Sabrina said, her gazed fixed on John's. "I left my bags in the car. Here," she told John, "take your shirt." She stepped toward him, the shirt slipping down her arms.

"Keep it," he whispered, laying a hand on her shoulders to stop her taking it off.

Not wanting anything from him, she shook her head in refusal. He did the same as he whispered, "Your uncle might not appreciate the view without the shirt."

Realizing that he was right and that he was once again taking care of her, Sabrina didn't know what to think. She turned back to her uncle. "I'm ready."

"John, Sabrina, what's happened to you guys? Breakfast is almost over."

"Sorry," they both mumbled. John immediately headed back inside the shelter.

"Kathy, this is my Uncle Darren. He's come from Lafayette to take me back to his home where my grandmother's staying."

"Nice to meet you. Why don't you stay for breakfast?"

"That would be a good idea, Uncle Darren," Sabrina suggested, figuring that he hadn't had time to stop and eat and feeling awful for nearly forgetting to say goodbye to the friends she had made in the last few days. "I'll drive so you can sleep," she offered.

"A meal does sound appealing," he said, stepping into the shelter behind them.

Sabrina said her goodbyes while her uncle ate, knowing that she wouldn't be able to stomach a bit of food. She avoided John, who seemed to be avoiding her.

She found her uncle standing in the doorway leading to the gym with Trooper Dan. He turned to her and said, "This is where you've been sleeping?"

"Actually, I've been sleeping up there." Sabrina pointed to the bleachers.

"Why?"

"Well, she had some company—"

"We just got cots yesterday morning," Sabrina interrupted, giving the trooper a hard look.

Either Uncle Darren hadn't caught it or had decided he didn't want to catch it because he turned to her and said, "Don't tell your grandmother."

"Of course not." Sabrina glanced once more at the bleachers, this time seeing John settle into their place, trumpet in had. "Let's go," she told her uncle, leaving the room before the beautiful sound of John's first love made its way to her ears.

CHAPTER 5

No time.

It had been four weeks since she'd come to Lafayette. That was twenty-eight days or six hundred seventy-two hours or forty thousand three hundred twenty minutes, however you wanted to look at it.

Whichever way she looked at it, Sabrina felt as if she hadn't had enough time.

Sabrina looked at the clock on the nightstand as it proclaimed that it was a few minutes before midnight. Where had the day gone?

There didn't seem to be time to deal with everything that had to be dealt with in the course of a day, which meant that she had no time to wallow in her disastrous interactions with John Lewis. Only during those few minutes before her brain retired for the night could she reflect on them. Her life was now consumed with Grammy, FEMA, the Red Cross and food stamps.

Food stamps!

Sabrina still couldn't believe that she had actually stood in line for food stamps. But necessity had forced her hand. Her grandmother was on a fixed income with no access to her monthly check that would have come at the first of September. And she didn't even have access to her little bit of savings. The credit union where her grandmother had always banked was local with no other branch outside the New Orleans area, translating into Grammy having no way to access her funds. Using the little money they had on hand, they opened a joint account with a bank with branches throughout the country, another event that took nearly all day with Grammy in tow. Too many other displaced New Orleanians were trying to do the same thing. As they stood in lines they shared their Katrina stories, speaking of their devastated neighborhoods and the slow rescue process in disbelieving tones.

Overall, Sabrina didn't feel that she was any help to her grandmother. Being a first year teacher she had just begun working in the public school system. She hadn't received her first paycheck and didn't know when or *if* she would.

Uncle Darren was terrific, but she couldn't expect her uncle to support them indefinitely.

So she had stood in line for food stamps so as to contribute something to the household.

Then she had stood in the unemployment line, having decided to forgo finding a job, too afraid to allow Grammy to stay home alone all day. Uncle Darren was barely home, working twelve, sometimes eighteen, hour shifts to fill the gap left by officers who had volunteered to help their fellow policemen in New Orleans.

Time.

How could she find the time to fix it all, to somehow make their world safe and sane once again. If only she could tuck away words like *devastated*, *displaced* and *evac-*

uees, words that seemed distant just a month ago, but had now become a part of her daily vocabulary.

"Are you just coming to bed, child?"

"Yes, Grammy." Sabrina lowered herself onto the bed she shared with her grandmother in her Uncle Darren's one and only guest room. A friend of his, a fellow evacuee, slept on the couch in the den and another friend on the floor.

"My poor baby, try to rest now. Things will come out all right in the end." A warm, shaky hand rested on Sabrina's shoulder.

"If you say so," Sabrina agreed because she knew it was what her grandmother wanted her to say. But she wondered about the many bumps, big and small, they would have to bounce over before reaching the outcome her grandmother predicted.

"I say so," Grammy whispered. Soon a soft snore indicated that she had fallen back to sleep.

As Sabrina lay in the bed, her body exhausted, her mind replayed every encounter she'd had with John from the concert in Mississippi until she left the shelter. Eventually she fell asleep.

The vibration woke her instantly. Sabrina quietly went into the kitchen, shutting off her phone's alarm. She quickly grabbed the cordless and dialed FEMA's number, which she by now knew by heart. For days that had turned into weeks she had tried to register her grandmother and herself as Hurricane Katrina victims. Wasted time. She'd spent the days dialing and redialing, hours on hold, only to get disconnected. Calling at midnight was one bright idea that she had had yesterday, only to discover that a whole lot of other people had had the same idea. But four o'clock in the morning? Most people would have just gone to bed or would still be sleeping. So, here she sat at the kitchen table at four o'clock in the morning calling FEMA and . . .

. . . and getting an answer.

Her spirits suddenly lifted. She was talking to a real human being. Sabrina found herself spilling her guts, telling her entire Katrina story before the woman could get one word in. "I'm sorry," fell out of her mouth when she had finally wound down. "I'm sure you've heard too many of these stories."

"It's quite all right. You probably needed to let some of it out of your system."

"I did," Sabrina said, realizing that she had kept a lot of her anxiety bottled up in an attempt to shield her grandmother. "Thanks."

For the next ten minutes she answered questions, providing her vital information so that emergency funds could be transferred. Sabrina felt as if a huge rock from the landslide that had fallen on her shoulders had been lifted, leaving her a draft of fresh air so that she could breathe a little easier.

The back door opened. Uncle Darren stepped in, stopping short when he saw her at the kitchen table. "You're either up mighty early or pretty late."

"Mighty early." Holding up the phone, she offered as a form of explanation, "FEMA."

"You finally got through?"

"Yes," she smiled.

"Smart girl."

It was good to hear the compliment. She hadn't felt very smart or resourceful, and since the incident Uncle Darren had witnessed with John, she was afraid that she had lost some respect in his eyes.

"That's nice to hear," she told him.

"It's the truth. You've done a fine job of helping your grandmother through all this. God knows I haven't had the time. Working and sleeping are all I've been doing."

"I know it seems that way, but you've also been providing us a roof over our heads."

"Family takes care of their own."

"And friends," Sabrina said, nodding in the direction of the den at the back of the house.

"Friends, too. They'll be getting back on their feet. They've both found a job and a place to stay in Shreveport."

"That far north?"

"Still in Louisiana, though."

When he didn't add any more Sabrina asked, "Would you like some coffee or tea? How about some breakfast?"

"No, just some sleep." He turned, heading toward his room.

"You know that I've grown up," Sabrina blurted, stopping him from walking out of the room.

"I couldn't help but notice."

Needing to say what had been in and out of her mind for the last month, Sabrina forged on. "What you saw at the shelter—between John and me—I hope you don't think I throw myself at any man I meet. I mean, it was John and I've loved him for such a long time . . ." she trailed off.

"Oh, so that's how it is?" he asked, slumping into a chair. " 'Cause, girl, you had me worried there."

At her nod he continued.

"I know you're grown and all but it's still hard to take seeing my little niece, my only niece, in certain situations, if you know what I mean."

"I do." Sabrina felt her face heat up.

"I wasn't going to tell you, but I saw him today."

"Him who? John?"

"Exactly who. He was playing his trumpet at the shelter near the university."

"Near UL? The University of Lafayette?"

"That's the one."

"What did he say? Did he ask about me? How long is he going to be in town?"

Realizing that she sounded like a love-sick groupie, Sabrina swallowed the next barrage of questions about how he looked and where he was staying.

"All I know is that he's been working through some jazz organization that's been setting up gigs for displaced musicians at shelters and schools."

"Anything else?"

A deep sigh rose from his chest. "I might be sorry I told you, and believe me, I don't want to know what you plan to do with this information, but he's going to be playing at a shelter in Opelousas. At the Yambilee building, if I remember that right."

"Yambilee," Sabrina repeated, her mind bouncing back and forth with a desire to see John and an aversion to another face-to-face encounter that could lead to more embarrassment.

"I see that this news has set your mind to thinking. Whatever you do, think smart. Goodnight."

"Goodnight," Sabrina absently responded, wondering if she had ever thought smart when it came to John. She shuffled back to bed, hoping to sleep an hour or two before Grammy woke up.

Sabrina woke up at seven-thirty, a full half hour earlier than her usual eight o'clock automatic wake up time. She'd usually find Grammy sitting in the den enjoying her favorite television show as she waited for her to wake up so that they could make breakfast together.

Maybe they'd get an earlier start, give them more time in the day, which could be useful if they decided to go to Opelousas, which happened to be about thirty minutes away. Sabrina went into the den. Uncle Darren's friends were gone, which wasn't unusual because they always got an early start, but the television was pitch black and Grammy was nowhere to be found. She checked every room in the house, leaving Uncle Darren's room for last.

Grammy wasn't known for sleepwalking, but that was in normal circumstances. Nothing was normal nowadays. What if she had developed an uncontrollable restlessness that led to sleepwalking and had been assaulted or even kidnapped right at the front door.

"Well, aren't you the early bird this morning?" the object of her sudden terror asked, as she shuffled through the kitchen door, her step a bit livelier than usual.

"Me?" Sabina started toward her grandmother to help her sit.

"Yes, you, and stay where you are. These seventy-eight-year-old bones can make it across the room and into that chair over there."

"Oh, you can."

"Most definitely. Those pills Darren's given me for my knees have made them almost as good as new."

"I can see that. Where have you been?" Sabrina asked, following her into the den.

"Where I've been every morning at this time. Next door, having a cup of tea with Faith before her daughter drags her off to that daytime old folks home. She can't stand the place."

"Faith. Who's Faith?"

"You know Faith, a friend of mine. She told me the most interesting thing today. There was a jazz concert at the shelter in town yesterday."

"Really?" Sabrina asked, trying to digest the fact that her grandmother had a new friend she knew nothing about and was feeling well enough to travel on her own, even though it was only next door, to visit with a friend. And exactly why didn't she know anything about Faith?

"Yes, really. Listen up, Sabrina Adams."

Without thinking, Sabrina sat up straighter. "I'm listening."

"Anyway, there's a Red Cross shelter in Opelousas off Highway 190. There'll be another concert there, and since we're evacuees I don't see why we can't enjoy some uplifting music. Besides, we could talk to the Red Cross people there in person to see what type of aid they have for us. My poor baby, you've been running yourself ragged trying to get things together. Your mind has been all over the place. You're so full of FEMA, insurance and housing that you're muttering about it all day long."

"No, that's not true."

"And even in your sleep."

"In my sleep?"

Grammy nodded and continued. "Do you know just how much worry I went through right after the hurricane when I didn't know exactly where you were? I made myself sick watching the television, thinking that message you sent was a little white lie to keep me from worrying and that you were in the Superdome or at the Convention Center."

"Oh, Grammy."

"I'm not saying this to make you feel bad or sorry for me. I'm saying this to make you focus."

"Focus?" Sabrina stood. Her face, she was certain, was the exact opposite of Grammy's sure, quiet expression. Sabrina was focused. She was focused on taking care of

Grammy, contacting the insurance company, and was so focused and diligent that she'd finally connected with FEMA, not to mention the food stamps and unemployment agencies.

"I meant that I want you to stop and focus on what's most important." Grammy took her hands and, with a firm tug, pulled her down so that she was kneeling before her. "For hours and hours, I watched, stunned, as our city sat in flood waters, as our people suffered. It was a hard thing to see. The streets that we'd walked—a million places you knew—the people you hoped had gotten away. It was all so terrible."

Grammy stopped and shook her head. Sabrina didn't fill in the silence with comforting words that would have interrupted her thoughts. It was obvious to her that Grammy needed to talk. Sabrina should have noticed before that Grammy had a ton of things on her mind and needed to get it all out.

"Darren tried to keep me away from it."

"The television?"

"Yes, but he was gone most of the time. Working. And there it sat, like a sore I couldn't let alone. But Sabrina, you have to know that there was something more that hurt even worse."

"What was that, Grammy?" Sabrina couldn't even begin to imagine what could be worse.

"Not knowing exactly where *you* were. Not seeing you with my own eyes and touching you, to know that you were safe. I sent you away to celebrate your birthday and I felt as if I'd sent you to your death-day. I didn't know if you had gotten out of harm's way or not."

"I tried to let you know," Sabrina started to explain. They hadn't talked about any of this in the last month. She had been too wrapped up in attempting to pull their lives back together again.

"That little message thing on that telephone? That wasn't enough for me. I needed to see you. It hurt my heart to see people suffering and to see our city drowning. It broke my heart in two to know that the home I bought with your grandpa and the place I raised your mama and Darren was destroyed. But just thinking," she paused to take a breath, "just thinking that I might have lost you in that mess, Sabrina, it tore at my *soul*."

"Oh, Grammy, I'm so sorry."

"I'm not. It was God's way of making me focus on what was really important in my life. Family. We've lost all of our material goods, and that's a huge pain and a burden to deal with. But the pain of losing it all was nothing compared to the thought of losing you."

"You haven't lost me. You've still got me."

"Well, almost."

"What do you mean by that?"

"Focus, Sabrina. Focus on what's really important. We're safe, we're alive."

"I get what you're saying," Sabrina stood, "but Grammy, there are things that need to be done."

"Not to the detriment of ignoring what's important. Don't let getting back on your feet knock you out of your shoes. Baby, most of the time I'm not sure you even know what's going on around you."

"Of course I do."

"Then you remember meeting Faith?"

"Aw, no. I've never met her and why haven't you told me about this tea time of yours?"

"I have. You're mind has been too full and—"

"—too focused on things important, but not the most important." Sabrina sighed, giving her grandmother a kiss. "So, you want to go to Opelousas?"

"Yes, so that you can take a minute for yourself."

"And a minute for you."

"Exactly, and I want to bring Faith along. I was coming to get you because I need you to talk to Faith's daughter, convince her to let Faith come with us for the day instead going to that daytime babysitter place."

Feeling a sudden change in the atmosphere and a definite bit of role reversal going on, Sabrina stalled with, "I don't know," as she adjusted herself to the situation that still seemed new, despite having found herself in the role of caretaker and decision maker a number of times before. "Exactly why would Faith's daughter not want her to go?"

"Because she's a worrywart."

"Grammy?"

"All right," Grammy said, easing herself out of her favorite chair. "Faith fell a few months ago, broke her hip and had to have surgery. She's recovered now and has to go to physical therapy twice a week. She's still a spring chicken, barely sixty-eight, and her daughter won't let her do a thing!"

"I understand."

"This would be a chance to focus our brains on something other than the misery Katrina's left us with."

"Think this little outing will help me refocus?"

"It's worth a try. Let's go talk to Diane before she leaves for work. That's Faith's daughter, just in case you forgot."

An hour later Sabrina found herself chauffeur to two giggling older ladies and on her way to a concert and John Lewis, who she had yet to decide she wanted to see.

Both women sat in the back chatting together like old friends, reminding Sabrina of the relationship her grandmother had had with Miss Joan, her high school girlfriend who'd died a little more than two years ago. It was good to hear her grandmother's voice filled with so much animation. It had been absent since the storm or maybe, because Sabrina had been so consumed with handling everything, she hadn't noticed one way or another. Whatever the case, if spending time with Miss Faith made her grandmother this happy, then Sabrina would make sure they spent more time together in the future.

The thirty-minute drive traveling north on Interstate 49 was a deliciously carefree moment desperately needed in the midst of their most recent experiences. In no time, it seemed, they had arrived, allowing her not a moment to worry about anything. It was refreshing to think of nothing beyond the moment, for however long it lasted.

Exiting the interstate they merged onto Highway 190, passing through the small town of Opelousas. Like so many of the towns, the central downtown area bustled with stores, businesses and houses, much the same as ones you would see in any city. Wanting to see more of the town, Sabrina took a detour. As she drove down one side street and then another, wide open spaces began to dominate the area, dotted with homes of many shapes and sizes, livestock, bales of hay here and there, and narrow roads with wide, deep ditches.

"Isn't this a peaceful place?" Grammy commented.

"Yes, mighty peaceful," Miss Faith agreed as Sabrina made a soft sound of agreement as she turned to make their way back to the highway and the Yambilee building. As soon as they parked in the gravel lot, Grammy's door swung open. She was out of the backseat and on the other side of the car opening the door for Miss Faith with the speed of someone half her age. The excitement in the air was a vibrating energy that hit Sabrina as soon as she opened her car door. People were dashing in and out of the large, gym-like structure. Everyone seemed to be talking in excited whispers.

Sabrina opened the trunk and removed the walker for Miss Faith. Convincing her daughter Diane to allow her mother to go on the trip had been a monumental task. She had eventually melted under the pressure of two old women and a multitude of promises made by Sabrina, half of which she couldn't remember.

Despite Miss Faith's use of the walker, the throbbing energy surrounding them quickened their steps. They found their way to the entrance in no time at all, only to be extremely disappointed.

"Good morning ladies. IDs ,please," a young gentleman smiled at them.

"We don't have IDs," Grammy said, in a pitifully soft voice.

"Then you're not residents?"

At the shake of their heads he paused regretfully before saying, "I'm sorry, ladies, but you have to be a resident to attend the concert."

"But we're hurricane victims, too," Miss Faith said.

"And we deserve a bit of spirit lifting," Grammy added.

"I'm sure that's true," the young man began.

"You can't mean to say that those who were lucky enough to find relatives to stay with are not welcomed?" Grammy continued.

The young volunteer released a big sigh. His mouth turned downward into a droop of disappointment as he responded, "I wish I could allow you in, but the rules are set up to protect the residents."

"Oh, we wouldn't want to put them at risk," Grammy commented.

"When you think about it, they are in a worse situation than us. They've got to sleep in a big wide-open space like that big old gym you've got in there with a bunch of strangers. We've got a home to live in, even though it's not our own. It's a home," Miss Faith added.

"Sorry, I wish . . ." The volunteer trailed off, desperately looking around him, obviously feeling bad about kicking sweet old ladies out the door and seeking some help in doing so.

"Can we listen out here?" Grammy asked, wearing the most helpless feel-sorry-for-me old lady look. "Maybe in that little corner over there? I'm sure the music would reach us and we'd be no trouble at all."

"I don't . . ."

"Of course you can't," a deep, pleasant voice answered. "You all will be sitting center stage so that I can get a good look at your smiling faces when I toot my horn."

"John!" Grammy exclaimed, throwing herself into his arms as if he were a lifeline. "Sabrina, it's John!"

"I see, Grammy," Sabrina answered, taking a step back, attempting to suppress the instantaneous, pulsating attraction that refused to allow her to psyche herself into believing that she didn't care about him.

Instead, she focused on Grammy, understanding all too well what her grandmother was feeling. Sabrina herself had reacted in much the same way to people from New Orleans that she had seen on the streets of Lafayette. A neighbor, her mailman, even a co-worker she had known for all of two weeks. Each person got a huge hug, a mini-evacuation survival story, an analysis of how homes fared or how they thought their homes had fared, depending on if they had even been allowed to get to them, and an update on how things *were* or *were not* going. It had become a ritual, a bond that helped a fellow evacuee go on. You felt as if you couldn't see, touch or talk to the other person enough.

Grammy's hand lay on John's shoulder and lingered there with an affectionate pat. It was a touch Sabrina wouldn't, couldn't feel comfortable giving because what she felt for John could not be measured or expressed by mere affection.

"So, how have you been? Where have you been? How'd you make out? Where's ya' mom and 'em?" Grammy asked, nearly all in one breath. Then, "Sabrina, can't you see John standing here? What's wrong with you? It's John! He's like family. He's the brother you never had. Give him a hug, say hello. Do something more than stand there."

At that moment her eyes connected with his. Sabrina wondered if they conveyed the something her imaginative mind had produced the instant she saw him. He didn't hold her gaze more than a second or two making Sabrina think that he could read her eyes well enough. *Do something more,* Grammy said. If only her grandmother knew what she had been thinking just now.

"Sabrina?"

"Grammy, she's not as surprised to see me. We spent time in the shelter together, remember?"

"You were with Sabrina in that shelter?"

"Yes, ma'am."

"I didn't know that. Why didn't I know that?"

Not knowing what to say, Sabrina looked from one to the other and then at Miss Faith, whose eyes had widened and whose head seemed to bob in three different directions. "Are you okay, Miss Faith?" she asked, responding to the safest situation.

"Red, time to blow," a slightly older man poked his head out the door to say.

"Red?" Sabrina asked.

"Nickname," John responded. "Like it?"

"No."

John shrugged. "It's time to go in. Let's get you settled. Jeff," John said to the silent volunteer, "these are my special guests. I can vouch for their character," he said. "I'd appreciate you finding a seat for them, somewhere in the front if you can manage it."

They didn't get to sit front row center, and honestly wouldn't have felt right taking that privilege from a resident of the shelter. A trio of chairs in the far corner of the room stood empty and appeared to be waiting expressly for them. The next hour was a nourishing, revitalizing therapy session. The shelter residents, fellow evacuees, all of them, were hungry for a taste of New Orleans. John, along with three other talented musicians, was providing necessary ingredients to feed bruised and battered souls.

A soft, jazzy beat.

A rousing march with the saints.

Some mellow tunes from home.

The concert was a sweet, flavorful meal.

After a very loud and long standing ovation that had Miss Faith tilting from one side of her walker to the other and Grammy about ready to fall backwards into her chair, the leader of the group got everyone's attention.

"I've got a story for you."

The shelter became silent.

"Now I know that you all have stories. Most with a rotten beginning and a dismal middle. But know this, these stories have not come to an end because we shall rise. We're coming back. Ain't that right, New Orleans?"

"Right!" the shelter vibrated.

"And to keep us going, we have a few inspiring chapters in our stories. We try to share a chapter or two as we visit with our family. You know you're our family, right?"

"Family!" someone shouted.

"Family!" the entire assembly shouted right back, Sabrina, Grammy and Miss Faith right along with them.

"Well, some chapters are darn right inspiring because they prove that we're stronger than we think we are, and sometimes we just need a little push or a bit of a reminder that we've got the inner strength to withstand anything. This story is a chapter in Red's life. Come up here, Red."

Sabrina watched as John walked forward center stage and stood smiling before the crowd. He was in his element. The stage was where he belonged. John radiated with an aura, the same exact shining light he emitted whenever he held a trumpet in his hands. The way he'd looked at her once. And exactly the way he looked at the concert in Mississippi.

That comfortable smile he used to wear when he spoke to her spread wide to charm the residents. As she listened, her mind traveled back to the moment he described to his audience. It was the day that they'd found out the levees had failed, allowing the city to drown. Sabrina was transported back to that surreal moment in time.

"To ease the pain of such devastating news I played my trumpet and this was the song I chose, 'Do You Know What It Means?' "

Closing her eyes, Sabrina imagined herself looking up into the bleachers, feeling a kinship with everyone there, especially John. As the song ended, Sabrina could almost feel John's heated gazed on her. When she opened her eyes he had moved back to stand with the other members of the band.

"Give it up for Johnny Red, our newest trumpet player."

John stepped forward and took a bow.

"Thank you. Hold on to your stories and keep adding chapters," John told the crowd. "They will get better and better and before you know it you, you won't be missing New Orleans because you'll be back there. See you in N'awlins!" he called, making everyone love him because he was John and he cared, truly cared, about the people he had just played for.

Grammy refused to leave without seeing him again, so they stayed in the back and watched as John and his fellow musicians walked through the crowd and spoke to the residents. His concern was evident in the amount of time he spent talking with the residents after the concert and couldn't go unnoticed since Grammy and Miss Faith expounded on his many virtues.

"Isn't he just a sweetie?"

"Not one of them ran off right after the concert."

"And they're not giving people the brush-off either."

"Yeah, none of that phony smile and a wave kinda thing."

"Nice young men."

"Oh, yes, especially our John. He comes from good people."

"Yeah."

"So down to earth a couple of 'em even married white."

"Grammy!"

"They did! Which just shows that skin don't matter. Good character's good character. His sister Vanessa and those two cousins of his, Daniel and Teresa, found that out. That girl Monica found herself a fine, black man with excellent character."

"Grammy!"

"Stop Grammying me and take a look at these nice, young handsome men who care about other people."

"I've noticed them, Grammy."

"I have too, Viola," Faith interjected.

"But our John's the most handsome," Grammy declared.

Sabrina nodded to appease her grandmother but stretched her neck to appease her growing need to simply look at him. He *was* one fine man. In body and spirit, Sabrina thought as he bent to pick up a toy for a toddler, his firm backside outlined in the jeans that were a wee bit too tight for him.

"Sabrina!"

"Sabrina Adams!" A tug on her arm made her realize that Grammy had been calling her while she stared holes into a backside she wished she had the freedom to touch.

"Yes, Grammy."

"Didn't you have a crush on John or was it Josh, his twin. There's another one out there just as handsome as him, Faith," Grammy turned to tell her friend. "Maybe it's both. They look exactly alike."

"Hi, Grammy," John said before Sabrina had a chance to answer.

"John, who did Sabrina have a crush on? You or Josh?"

As Sabrina did her best to look everywhere but at his beautiful eyes he answered, "Both."

"A crush on *you*!" Sabrina turned in time to see the sax player elbow John in the ribs. "If you introduce me to these beautiful ladies I guarantee that before they leave everyone will have crush on *me*!"

Sabrina smiled, the crack relieving the tension Grammy's remark had caused. She hadn't even realized that Grammy knew about her crush. And to announce it to John and his band the way she did had Sabrina wondering if the after-effects of the storm had tossed her brains around a bit.

The musicians chatted with them for a while, even escorted them to the car.

"John, you haven't told me a thing about your family," Grammy asked. "How have they made out?"

"That's a lot of information to tell. You know there are a lot of us."

"Then come have dinner with us, all of you. It'll do an old woman some good to be surrounded by a bunch of handsome men. Faith lives next door so she'll be there, too."

"We've got a duet tonight," the sax and trombone player declined.

"I've got to see about my mama tonight," the other trumpet player announced.

"I—" John paused and looked at Sabrina as if seeking permission to come or stay away. Whatever he read in her eyes prompted him to say, "—would love to visit with you all."

He helped Grammy into the backseat. The trombone player helped Miss Faith and the sax player placed the walker in the trunk.

"Darren's house is easy to find."

While Grammy was giving John directions, the leader, a man about three or four years older than John, leaned into the open window of the car. "If you're all done with that crush on Red, I hope you don't mind me asking if you'd be interested in getting to know this trumpet player."

Sabrina knew her eyes must have turned to saucers because he immediately added, "I don't mean to scare you. I'm not a weirdo, just a man looking for a nice woman to spend some time with, and if Red's not interested—"

"Why do you call him Red?" Sabrina asked, her way of dealing with a situation she did not want to handle. She had way too much to handle already.

"You are from New Orleans, right?"

"Yes."

"I find it strange that you have to ask. Light-skinned brother . . ."

"Oh, I knew that."

"Johnny Red fit."

"It does."

"And you're still hung up on him?"

"I'm afraid so."

"Then I'll wish you good luck and do you a quick favor. How about a little something to make him jealous?"

"A little something?"

"A quick kiss, in a friendly sort of way. But of course, I won't let on that it's friendly."

"What?" Sabrina was saying as she turned her head to look directly at him. He was leaning into the car. The kiss he was attempting to land on her cheek fell onto her lips. It was a soft, sweet kiss that stirred not a bit of excitement in her blood.

He leaned back, both hands still clenching the door, a meaningful expression on his face. "The name's James. Let me know if it doesn't work out."

"Sure," she whispered, starting the engine.

"Why were you kissing a man you barely know?" Grammy was asking her.

"I wasn't kissing him, he was kissing me. If it were up to me I would have been kissing John."

"So you still do have a crush on him."

"More like a love for him," Sabrina admitted.

"Well, I'll be," Grammy said.

"We'll all be," Sabrina said, noting the angry stance and the way John's face turned to James and then the car. "We'll all be wondering if it means anything at all." Peeking at her rearview mirror she saw John following James with a purposeful stride. It might end up meaning something, Sabrina thought, driving through Opelousas, knowing she'd consider it an interesting chapter in her own story.

CHAPTER 6

"Why don't you have some more dirty rice? Sabrina made it herself!" Grammy declared as she added a heaping spoonful to John's plate, making the suggestion a done deal.

Sabrina avoided glancing at the opposite end of the table where John was penned in by Grammy and Miss Faith. Sabrina shared a look of exasperation with her uncle sitting beside her.

"Put another piece of chicken on his plate, Faith," Grammy was saying. "Sabrina had a hand in cooking the chicken, too. And don't give me that look, John. What man can get full on one little chicken leg?"

"No man but me, obviously," Uncle Darren answered, raising an eyebrow at Sabrina. Then his gaze moved to his empty plate and traveled to the women fawning over John.

"Darren, don't be foolish. You're not company. Help yourself!" Grammy ordered, proceeding to praise the various wonders of the yams Sabrina had also had a hand in making.

Funny, all Sabrina remembered doing was taking them out of the pantry. Grammy might as well have given credit to the farmers who planted the sweet potatoes and the soil, rain and sun that made them grow. Maybe even the earthworms—

"Diane's company!" Uncle Darren's voice broke into Sabrina's rambling thoughts, evidence that he hadn't let go of the fact that John was getting way too much attention. "I don't see anybody hovering over her or filling her plate. She must feel left out."

"He's right—" John began but Sabrina seemed to be the only person to hear him because Grammy continued her quest of filling his plate and Diane was in a heated discussion with her mother.

"Pay no attention to him, John. See what you did, Darren! Making John feel uncomfortable and all, and after losing everything to Katrina, shame on you."

"We all lost everything to Katrina—" John began, attempting to stop Grammy from adding another spoonful of dirty rice, sprinkled with the essence of Sabrina, of course, to his plate.

Sabrina sat back to watch the scene play out, finding herself entertained despite her initial exasperation.

"He's right," Uncle Darren agreed. "And I don't think somebody should have to lose a home from a hurricane to get some hospitality around here. I think somebody ought to be paying attention to Diane. Look, her plate's still empty." He grabbed Diane's plate and began to pile it high with every dish on the table. The overflowing plate landed in front of Diane with a clank that filled the room, drawing everyone's attention.

"Eat every bit of this food because somehow Sabrina managed to dip her magical fingers into every dish. Right, Sabrina?"

"The second after each and every one was made," Sabrina agreed.

Everyone laughed, diffusing the tension and the obvious embarrassment John was feeling with all the attention he'd been given evolving into a whole different kind of tension as the meal progressed. John darted a series of looks her way between replies and conversation with Grammy and Miss Faith, who was now ignoring her daughter.

The first look John tossed her way yelled, "Help!" which Sabrina ignored, figuring he deserved what he was getting. Then he tossed a thoughtful expression her way, followed by one of concern, which almost immediately narrowed into irritation, all the while conversing with the older women at his end of the table.

Sabrina wondered if his irritation had anything to do with being smothered by Grammy and Miss Faith or, she hoped, a result of James and his *favor*.

Was that completely un-stirring kiss James had given her on John's mind? If that was the case, then he had a nerve.

"Do you plan on eating any of this food," Uncle Darren asked, "or is it too full of—"

"Me?" Sabrina finished, poking at the tiny pieces of chicken livers and gizzards that was the *dirt* in her dirty rice. "Something like that," she answered, tearing her eyes away from the object of her annoyance.

Her uncle nodded, shifting his attention to Diane, who didn't seem to be too happy. As a matter of fact, she hadn't seemed to be too pleased to be here from the moment she had stepped into the house. "It wasn't my intention to offend your independent nature by filling your plate," he said to Diane between clenched teeth. "Would you like a clean one?" he asked after a slight pause.

"No, thank you," Diane ground out between tight teeth and tense lips.

Ohhh, something was brewing between the two of them, Sabrina was sure, but she didn't have enough room in her brain to speculate on the exchange with her mind so full of John and every bit of uncertainty she was experiencing in her life because of Hurricane Katrina. Staring at her nearly empty plate, she methodically added bits of everything else if for no other reason than to keep the dirty rice company. Chicken, yams, fresh green beans and a roll stared at her with a promise of being delicious despite her sudden distaste for the meal. The feeling was completely foreign to her because Sabrina loved food. And growing up in New Orleans had added a deeper dimension to her appreciation of good Creole cooking.

As the meal progressed the odd tension coming from Uncle Darren and Diane bombarded Sabrina, who was literally caught between them. More tension was emitted from John via the irritated looks he continued to direct at Sabrina. Oblivious to the tension Grammy and Miss Faith chatted away, extolling John's many virtues.

Grammy began, "John, there are a few things you don't know about my one and only granddaughter—"

Sabrina quickly interrupted. "Grammy, what's for dessert?"

"Dessert? Faith and I baked up a peach cobbler."

"It's the least we could do. After all, Sabrina cooked the entire meal all—"

"I'll get the cobbler." Sabrina popped up and was in the kitchen before Grammy could utter a sound.

"Why are you so worried about dessert when you haven't eaten a bite?" Grammy's voice reached her in the kitchen where Sabrina had successfully escaped the listing of her many virtues, meant to point out to John what a good catch she was. John was smart enough to know what a good catch she was but too foolish and way too stubborn and too wrapped up in his music to even notice, let alone reach for a good woman who loved him and—

Ah, what was the use? Remembering her reason for escaping to the kitchen, Sabrina scanned the kitchen but couldn't find any evidence of a dessert. Not even the sweet peachy smell of one of her favorites.

Going to the oven, Sabrina opened it just as Grammy came through the door asking, "What's taking you so long?"

"Well, if it's dessert you want, it's going to take a whole lot longer than the five minutes it took to find it."

"Oh, did I leave it in the oven?"

"Yes, in the cold oven."

"You mean I didn't even turn it on? And I was just promising John a sweet ending to his meal. We have to get that man a dessert."

"What's going on?" Miss Faith popped into the kitchen.

"We forgot to turn the oven on," Grammy answered, looking more distressed than the situation called for. Could dealing with the immense tragedy caused by Katrina cause small problems to seem bigger? Sabrina knew that, emotionally, they were all reacting to the many major changes in their lives differently. Could this be a warning sign indicating that Grammy needed to be watched more closely?

"Oh, and John was so looking forward to something sweet," Miss Faith was saying with a great deal of drama. "Why don't you two young people go out and pick up some ice cream?" she suggested, her voice a sugary plea.

Sabrina's eyes went from one to the other, suspicious of this much too convenient excuse to throw her and John together, especially since Miss Faith had given the suggestion. Grammy knew that Sabrina was less likely to balk at a suggestion made by her new friend. Add that to Grammy's blessings on the idea of Sabrina and John as a couple, which had been repeatedly given during the entire thirty minute ride back to Lafayette after the concert, as well as the opinion that they were perfectly matched. These two old women were up to some serious matchmaking.

"The oven is now on and the cobbler is baking. We'll just have to wait for it to finish."

"And what will we do till then, smarty pants?" Grammy asked, none too happy with the way things were going.

"Find a way to entertain our guest."

"I got it!" Grammy's face lit up. "When Darren came to get me before the storm I packed a suitcase full of photo albums. We could look through those!"

"You have our albums, Grammy?" Sabrina asked in a small voice, having already mourned the loss of the precious memories of her youth and her mom, who had died when she was barely two years old. Sabrina had never brought the subject up, thinking that the loss would cause Grammy to relapse.

"And every picture that hung on the wall. Darren helped to pack them all. I had a feeling that I needed to take them with me."

Sabrina gave Grammy a hug. "I'm glad you listened to yourself."

"Me, too. I even went into your room and packed the picture of you and your mama that sat by your bed."

"Thanks, Grammy." Sabrina could feel her throat tightening and become raw with tears she didn't want to shed.

"Come on, Faith, and help me get them out of the suitcase. We can have a laugh or two while the dessert's baking."

"Grammy, wait!" Sabrina stood in front of her grandmother, a hand on each shoulder, blocking her way out of the kitchen. "I'm thrilled that you've saved our pictures but if you take those out right now all your matchmaking efforts will go down the toilet."

"Matchmaking?"

"Yes, matchmaking. And if you really want us to get together then you had better not pull out those albums. John will just look at me as a kid again."

"A kid? But you're a beautiful woman," Miss Faith said, looking her up and down as if to confirm what she already knew.

"Of course she is," agreed Grammy. "He's not seeing it, huh?"

"He's not wanting to."

"Then why don't we ask John to play his trumpet?" Miss Faith suggested.

"Oh, no!" Sabrina said, nipping that idea in the bud. She didn't think she could stand to watch John gaze at the instrument with his usual love and devotion when she was feeling deprived of the very thing he lauded on his trumpet. "That wouldn't be fair to John. Why don't we ask Uncle Darren and Diane to get the ice cream?"

"Step away from my chair. I'm skipping dessert." Diane's voice burst into the room. A scrape of a chair and few footsteps later she peeped into the kitchen to say, "Thanks for dinner," directing the polite phrase to the kitchen in general. "Call me when you're ready to come home, Mama," she told Miss Faith, who nodded in reply.

"That idea's gone out the window," Grammy muttered.

"Don't worry about it. John and I will go, *if* you two stop matchmaking. I'll handle John."

"You're going to get the ice cream?"

"Only if you promise to let me deal with John in my own way, and in my own time."

"Sure," they answered together.

Sabrina entered the dining room just in time to see Diane glare at Darren before turning away. He stared holes in her retreating back, fists clenched tight as he muttered something under his breath before pushing away from the table and heading to his room.

"Those are the two you should be practicing your matchmaking skills on."

"Darren?" Grammy asked.

"And Diane?" Miss Faith squeaked.

Sabrina nodded, walking over to John, suddenly excited about the prospect of being alone with him.

"There seems to have been a mishap with the dessert. Do you want to take a ride with me to get a replacement?"

"Sure." John jumped out of his chair. Sabrina wondered what had him moving the fastest. His need to get away from the smothering attention of Grammy and Miss Faith, or to escape the lingering tension left behind by Darren and Diane. Or was the purposeful glint in his eye an indication that he had his own reasons for jumping at the chance for the two of them to be alone. This was going to be an interesting ride.

"Well, isn't that nice?" Miss Faith was saying as she and Grammy walked back into the dining room.

"We'll start cleaning up here while you two get the ice cream." Grammy saw them to the door.

"Ice cream?' he asked, holding the door open for her.

Sabrina nodded, walking through the front door ahead of him, more than curious to see what all those faces he'd made during dinner meant. What questions would come out of his mouth? Would they have anything to do with James and the favor he had bestowed on her in the Yambilee parking lot after the concert?

"Have a nice ride," Miss Faith called out.

"Go to the ice cream shop on Johnston Street. They've got the best ice cream," Grammy called out, directing them to drive past at least three grocery stores and another ice cream shop in order to get to the one she suggested.

Sabrina smiled as she got into John's car, realizing that Grammy just couldn't help herself.

"So." The one syllable hung in the air long after John started the engine and backed out of the driveway.

"So," he said again, driving down the street.

"Soooo? Sabrina asked, wanting him to supply more words to fill in the suddenly uncomfortable tension, worse than the one that had existed right after she had thrown herself at him.

"So," he said again. This time the word held a firm ring of determination. "What the hell did you think you were doing hanging halfway out of the window kissing James like your life depended on it?"

Sabrina had wanted more words but wasn't prepared for the tone of these. John had never spoken to her with what sounded like jealousy before. Hope raced through her blood, increasing her heart rate. Not wanting to get her hopes up, she took a deep breath and asked, "So, that bothered you?"

"Of course it bothered me. Something about it should have bothered you."

"And what would that be?" Sabrina asked, disappointed because she had to dig deeper. She wanted to get out of this weird stage in which they were stuck. John's next words had her hopes dropping downward a notch or two because his mind had meandered in a completely different direction from where she had hoped he was headed.

"It was right in front of your grandmother, Sabrina!"

"And *that* really bothered you?"

"Yes."

"Nothing else? No other little thing about the situation concerned you in any way, shape or form?"

John stopped at a red light and looked into her face. "You claimed to care about me."

"Tell me the truth, John. That's what got to you the most, didn't it?"

"What?"

It was so unusual to see such deep confusion run across his face that Sabrina couldn't reply to his question. She just sat there with a question of her own in her eyes.

"Yes," he ground out a full minute later. A horn blew, forcing him to realize that the light had changed. He drove on, the jerky way he handled the wheel some indication that he was not happy admitting as much as he had. He pulled into a gas station and parked at a pump. "What's happening to you, 'Brina?" he turned to ask.

Sabrina stared into his handsome face, so familiar and dear to her, and for the first time she saw more than a glimpse of the attraction she had been looking for. But the question he had thrown at her gave her only a second's worth of joy. It should have been, "What's happening to *us*?" Sabrina could feel another rejection coming on as John's voice repeated the question inside her head. It rolled into her very core, twisting inside her stomach before her mouth poured out an honest answer that had nothing to do with them.

"What's happened to me, you ask?" she began in a pleasant voice that Sabrina knew rang false. "Most recently, a heck of a lot has happened to me. Let's see, I was forced to evacuate my city, which has been devastated by a natural disaster. Devastated!

"I hadn't truly understood that word until recently, and it's been used so much I *feel* devastated just hearing it. And my devastated home is the only one I've ever known, by the way, the place where my mother was born and raised. It's the only real connection I have to her. It *could* be flooded with up to eight feet of water but I've got no idea because I haven't been allowed back despite the fact that we've been gone for almost two months. Oh, but I get to see vivid pictures on almost every news channel nonstop. I have lost the first real job I've ever had, making real money for the first time to help Grammy out. I haven't even seen my first paycheck. And you know what else, John? Do you know what else? I stood in line for *food stamps*! *Food stamps*! Just to contribute something to in the household. Oh, and of course, I've most recently thrown myself at you, spilling my guts about how I feel and getting rejected because I finally got the nerve."

"I didn't reject you," John said in a voice much harder and much deeper than his normal gentle timber.

"What do you call telling me that I didn't know my own mind and that your music was the most important thing in your life?"

"I'd call that . . ." He let it hang between them.

"A spade." Sabrina finished for him.

"What?"

"Call a spade a spade. It's called rejection. You don't want me and I have to accept that and the fact that you don't care about me."

"I never said that. I have— I mean, I do have— I didn't realize how much until I saw you hanging out the window locking lips with James!" he finally got out with great difficulty.

"Oh." Sabrina said into the sudden silence.

"He's a player, you know."

"Oh," Sabrina said again. A few seconds later, she felt John's hand on her shoulder. His touch relayed comfort and warmth and a bit of reassurance she hadn't realized that she needed.

" 'Brina, I know things have been tough. We've all been through more than we ever expected in a lifetime. Everyone's reality has been changed. We'll make our way back to it, maybe even make a better one. You're strong, and to hear Grammy talk, you've been handling things really well. Don't let this situation and your anger at me drive you to get involved with James."

"I'm not. I wasn't. You know me better than that, John," Sabrina said, peering up at him. "At least I thought you did. James said he was doing me a favor." Her eyes widened as she finally took in his earlier admission. "Did you just say that you care about me, or am I asleep at the kitchen table on hold for FEMA?"

"Doing you a favor? What kind of favor?" were the only words that John latched onto.

Sabrina shrugged her shoulders. "You'd have to ask James. Now, back to the caring thing. How do you care for me?"

"What do you mean *how*?

"Like a sister? A friend?" Sabrina paused before asking, "A lover?"

Silence.

"Well?" Sabrina asked in exasperation as he hesitated, his fingers gripping the steering wheel, a good sign, but far from enough.

"The last one."

"Oh." Sabrina smiled inside despite his lack of enthusiasm.

"I didn't want this."

Her lips twisted in agreement. "That's obvious."

"That came out wrong. It has nothing to do with you."

"I'd say it has everything to do with me."

"Not my reaction. Sabrina, you are a gorgeous, wonderful person who I never expected to be attracted to."

"This started out sounding pretty good, but now I'm hoping for it to improve, so keep going."

"I'd have never thought that a look from you or that lopsided smile of yours when I say something completely ridiculous would be . . ."

"Would be what?"

"Sexy as hell, and that I'd want to curve your lips into something other than a smile."

Sabrina's lips automatically turned into that lopsided grin. "What's stopping you?"

He seemed to give serious thought to the question before responding with, "Not a thing." John leaned across the console, and his fingers wrapped around her neck to pull her toward him.

A sigh full of a dozen different feelings escaped her lips just before John took them, pulling her soft breath inside him. Searching with his tongue, John found the heated longing that she couldn't suppress. He pulled back, his eyes briefly conveying the awe inspired by the mere joining of their mouths. He came back for more and Sabrina wallowed in the texture of his tongue against hers, freely given, freely roaming, intensifying the thrill because John wasn't simply reacting to a surprise kiss. He was expressing how he felt about her. He was letting go, giving in to *them.*

If it were possible to melt, a liquefied version of herself would be spread across the seat. But she was solid and charged. Her body was pulsating beneath her clothes, and a throbbing wetness between her thighs was a sign of how one kiss from John could turn her into nothing more than want and need.

Before he slowly pulled away from her, he drew her lower lip into his mouth, his tongue caressing the softness of her inner lip before releasing it. Their breathing was a harsh sound in the silent car, echoing their desire for more, driving them back together, demanding and taking with urgent stokes before easing into a gentleness to be savored. They lingered over the sweet connection of tongue, lips and, finally, the simple press of foreheads as their breathing subsided into an even rhythm.

A horn blew somewhere outside, invading their world. Their eyes locked and held. Neither seemed able to look away. Relief flooded through Sabrina. Regret was totally absent.

A knock on the window pulled them apart. Sabrina leaned against the seat as John rolled down the window.

"Mister, if you're not going to buy gas, then you have to move away from the pump. There's a line. I've never seen so many people here before all those evacuees arrived."

"No problem. I'll move," John answered, starting the engine and quickly pulling out of the gas station.

"So what now?" Sabrina asked, her mind on the many 'what nows' they could be heading to.

"Ice cream," he answered. His mouth curved into a mischievous, sexy grin.

"Besides the ice cream."

"In that case, we take one step at a time."

Being completely dissatisfied when it looked as if that was all he had to say, Sabrina added, "And that first step would be?"

"You want specifics?" he asked, turning to face her as he stopped at another red light.

His voice was deadpan but his eyes were full. Full of—. Sabrina couldn't think of a word to describe what she saw in his eyes, only that she was relieved to see it. "Yes, John, I want there to be at least one area in my life where I know where I'm headed."

"And you're sure you want to head there with me?"

"Yes, and I'm getting pretty tired of telling you this."

"Then we step into getting to know each other in a whole new light," he said, pulling into the driveway of the ice cream shop.

"Sounds like a step in the right direction." Sabrina leaned across the console to prove the truth of that statement.

CHAPTER 7

"It's Uncle John! It's Uncle John!" an excited little girl called before Sabrina and John could make it to the front door of a large, newly constructed two-story house.

"And he's got a girlfriend?" a young, masculine voice said in a loud whisper.

"A *girlfriend*?" the first voice shrieked in horror. If Sabrina had guessed right was it was one of John's little nieces.

"Uncle John doesn't have a girlfriend, that's just Sabrina," said another voice, who Sabrina immediately recognized as belonging to Jasmine, Jazz for short, another one of the many nieces and nephews who were now surrounding them.

Sabrina expected John to contradict the statement but in the next instant, they were swallowed by a sea of open arms and welcoming greetings as they were ushered into the house. Somehow separated from John, Sabrina found herself being gushed over by Vanessa and Monica, two of John's sisters and mothers to most of the kids hopping all over John.

"Ahhhh!" roared a big man Sabrina knew to be John's dad. "Get away from my son, you little rascals. I need to see if Katrina blew off any body parts that might be important."

The kids, used to their grandfather's antics, giggled and dashed toward Sabrina. Since she had been their regular babysitter for a couple of years, they had a ton of questions to ask.

"Did you finish college yet?" Jazz wanted to know.

"Are you a teacher now?" Tony piped in.

"Did your classroom get blown away by Hurricane Katrina?" Mark whooshed away from her in demonstration.

"Ours did," Megan supplied, "and now we're going to a new school and we live here in Gonzales with Auntie Monica and Uncle Devin and Maw-Maw and Paw-Paw. We have sixteen people living here. It's 'cause all of our houses were flooded by Katrina!"

"That's quite enough, Megan," Ness told her stepdaughter, whose blue eyes had gotten bigger and bigger as she relayed the information. "You kids, go on outside and play. We'll call you in later for dinner." Turning back to Sabrina, Ness offered her a seat as Monica followed the kids outside, issuing clear and precise instructions on what they could and could not do. "Sorry about that. I think Megan's dealing with the situation by sharing as much information as she can with anyone who will listen."

"At least she's getting it out of her system."

"That's what I've been thinking," Ness answered, launching into a few questions of her own. "How have you been? What has it been, a whole year since I've seen you? And how did John find you? I had no idea that you were coming but it's a wonderful surprise to see you."

As Monica joined them, Sabrina began answering Ness's questions on automatic pilot. She couldn't stop herself from glancing at John periodically. After he'd finished talking to his dad, his mom had come over to engulf him in a tight hug. Any minute now he would call her over to say, "Mom and Dad, do you remember Sabrina? She's my girlfriend," or at the very least, "Remember Sabrina? We're dating now." But neither happened. John was captured by his two his brothers-in-law with a welcome almost as loud as that of the kids and a demand that he show them how to repair a glitch on their computer.

Sabrina hoped her disappointment didn't show on her face. She was genuinely happy to see Ness and her family again. Ness was the best neighbor a teenage girl without any siblings could have had. Her frustration was once again with John. After their return to Darren's house with dessert, John had invited her to come see his family who were temporarily living in Gonzales, Louisiana, about an hour's drive southeast of Lafayette. Sabrina had taken that as a sign that not only had he acknowledged his feelings for her, but was ready to acknowledge a relationship. Sabrina had already shared the news with Grammy, who had probably broadcast it to the entire neighborhood.

Some acknowledgement. He hadn't even told his family that she was coming with him. And she hadn't realized that this was the first time he had seen any of his family since before Katrina. Sabrina began to feel out of place, as if she were intruding.

"And you both took the wrong exit and ended up at the same shelter?" Monica was asking just as Joyce and Calvin Lewis, John's parents, came to join them.

They were a handsome couple, their coloring on opposite ends in a spectrum of browns. Mr. Calvin was a deep chocolate and Miss Joyce a caramel color.

"Joycie, I'm heading out to keep an eye on those kids," John's father bellowed to the room, despite addressing his wife directly.

"Thank you, Calvin," she answered.

"Don't let them wear you out, Dad," Ness advised.

"As if they could," he answered, storming toward the door.

Taking a seat, Joyce Lewis said, "So you and John ended up at the same shelter? We were so worried about him being away and all when it was discovered how close the storm was going to hit. We had thought it was heading to Florida until the last minute. We couldn't call him with the phones being so congested and all, and we had no idea if he had been forced to stay in the city. We imagined him possibly suffering at the Superdome, like so many people. It was difficult enough to watch people we didn't know, and to think of any of my children in the middle of that mess . . . It was hard to deal with knowing that Randy, being a policeman and all, had to stay."

"We know, Mom," Monica said, no one needing to add more. They all sat in silence remembering vigils in front of the television not for hours, but for *days,* watching fellow New Orleanians unlucky enough to be trapped in the city.

The silence was interrupted by small feet pounding past the den and into the kitchen a few seconds later.

"Mark, who is that for?" Monica asked her son.

"Paw-Paw. He needed something to drink." Mark, who looked to be about seven years old, held up an ice-cold bottle of water. "Gotta go, Paw-Paw's *dying* of thirst."

"At least he didn't send the child in for beer," Joyce said, as Mark bounded out the door.

They all laughed, breaking the sad tension that had fallen over them in remembrance of the slow response for help after Katrina had flooded most of the city.

"And how is your grandmother?"

"Doing fine, Miss Joyce," Sabrina answered, relating Grammy's evacuation story. They in turn shared theirs, which involved over twenty hours on the road in traffic that moved no more than five miles an hour for the sixty-five miles to Baton Rouge. Since they couldn't make it to Houston as they had planned, they settled for a hotel room in Baton Rouge. They stayed there for over a week before finding, and buying, this newly constructed house in Gonzales, a few miles southeast of Baton Rouge. Sabrina knew Scott and Devin owned their own construction company and were well off, but to be able to buy a brand new house outright? They were definitely some of the fortunate ones; some people were still living in hotel rooms, if they were lucky. Sabrina wouldn't be surprised if they were living a dozen or more to a room. Many were still in shelters like the one she and John had stayed in during the storm.

"Megan's still amazed at sharing a house with sixteen people. She obviously doesn't remember sharing a hotel room and one bathroom at first."

"I don't think she noticed," Monica said. "That week was a blur of intense emotion and if we hadn't had each other, we would have all fallen into despair."

"It's sounds a little corny, but it's the truth," Ness agreed.

"It's true. I had John at the shelter to lean on, and just having Grammy and Uncle Darren afterward has made it possible to stay—"

"Sane." Miss Joyce finished.

"Exactly!" everyone agreed.

Another set of footsteps and a blur of yellow dashed by, followed by a glimpse of red.

"Vicki," Ness called out to her stepdaughter.

"Jazz," Monica called out to her own daughter.

Slower footsteps made their way back.

"Yes?" they asked in unison. They were both about nine years old by now, Sabrina guessed.

"If you wake up the babies we are going to put you both down for a nap," Ness warned.

Jazz's eyes widened and Vicki shook her head from side to side, her blonde ponytail swaying back and forth.

"You may go quietly, but I first need to know *where* you're going."

"Well, Paw-Paw needed his hat and sunglasses. He said he doesn't want his bald head to get sunburnt, but he's already too brown to get sunburnt, MaNessa." Vicki laughed. "But he doesn't believe me."

"And he's starving because Maw-Maw only gave him one piece of fish on his po-boy for lunch, so I have to get him a snack," Jazz explained.

"You two wait right here, girls," Joyce told her grandkids. She left the room, returning with a baby bonnet, an oversized pair of sunglasses, and an apple. "Tell him Maw-Maw sent him these things."

The girls giggled and turned to go outside. "Wait, Jazz. MaNessa, please don't call the boys and my cousins babies. They are getting to be big kids now and can run almost as fast as the rest of us." Then they dashed away, excited about their offerings to their grandfather.

"Vicki's right, isn't she?" Sabrina asked, realizing that the last time she had seen them, Ness's twin boys were walking and Monica's triplets were pulling up about ready to do the same.

"Unfortunately, yes. Ness's boys are three and mine will be three in a few months. She's also right about the running part. These kids are so fast it's scary."

"Good thing we have one adult for each toddler," Devin, Monica's husband, said as he came into the room. Three little ones made a beeline for Monica, crashing into her lap. She immediately began tickling them, genuinely happy to see them after a few hours' absence. Devin scooped a boy under each arm. Their giggling faces were tiny replicas of their dad's.

"That's Aaron and Chance," Monica told Sabrina. "And there's Blaze standing on her daddy's foot ready to go for a ride." Monica and Devin's little girl was a perfect combination of the two. Determined not to be left behind, she was bouncing on her daddy's foot and hanging on for dear life a second later as he began to move.

"Bathroom," Devin announced.

"I better go give Devin a hand," Monica said, following him to the back of the house.

Just then Scott, Ness's husband, and John came into the room. "Kacey and Kyle are still asleep?"

"Like little lambs," Scott said, a burst of laughter following the answer.

"What kind of lambs?" Ness asked as she stood putting a finger to her lips.

"Laughing lambs," John answered.

John and Scott twisted around, revealing two little boys hanging down their backs, the boys' ankles held securely by their dad and uncle.

"The blood will rush to their heads!" Ness said.

"It'll only make them smarter," Scott said.

"Release my children or you will suffer the consequences," Ness warned.

"Aw, Mommie," one curly-headed little boy moaned as Scott righted his son.

"That was fun, Uncle John," the other one said, bouncing up and down.

"Bathroom," Ness said, ushering them to the opposite part of the house.

Sabrina was trying to catch John's eyes to share in the fun all around them, wanting to give him some indication that she was having a good time and was really enjoying his family. But he seemed to be looking in every direction but hers.

Devin returned with the boys and was now standing next to Sabrina. "John," he called out, giving John no choice but to look in her direction. Just as his head turned, the room exploded with laughter.

"Joycie!" Calvin Lewis bellowed at the front door, five giggling kids bouncing all around him. "What's the meaning of this?" There stood John's dad, a frilly bonnet barely covering his bald spot and tied in place under his nose and huge sunglasses dominating his face. "Well?" he said, taking a giant bite out of his apple.

Cameras and camera phones were pulled out to snap the ridiculous picture he made. Sabrina was standing right behind John when he snapped his dad's picture and turned to say something to Ness. His eyes collided with hers and Sabrina knew the love she had for him was plain to see. A brief reflection of what she was feeling flashed at her, only to be replaced with something Sabrina did not care to name.

Not allowing her disappointment to show, Sabrina said to the room in general, "I almost forgot the pralines Grammy made." She walked out the door, leaving the fun and laughter of the tight-knit family the Lewises had always been, to come to the realization that she would never have what Ness and Scott, Monica and Devin, Miss Joyce and Mr. Calvin had, not with John. Even though he had taken a step forward with her, today he had retreated back at least a dozen steps. Life was too short, and uncertain, to hang onto someone who didn't know what he wanted. She deserved better than that, Sabrina decided, unlocking the door and plopping into the passenger seat. Leaning forward, she reached her hands beneath the seat searching for the plastic container that she had tucked there this morning. She was surprised to see a tear land on her arm. Wiping her eyes, she sat up.

"I wanna go for a ride!" One of Ness's boys patted her on her leg and was already hopping into her lap without waiting for a reply.

"You little rascal!" Ness said a few feet behind him. "Sorry about that, Sabrina. Kyle figures if someone's leaving the house then he needs to be with them."

"Please." He turned to face Sabrina, trying to plead his case with an adorable tilt of his head before his mother reached them. Then he laid it on thick by giving her a hug, his tiny arms encircling her neck and squeezing for dear life.

"You little charmer. Get down this instant, Kyle Hallowway," Ness said in a firm tone.

Realizing that his mom meant business, he looked from Sabrina to Ness before saying, "Don't cry," giving Sabrina a kiss before hoping out of the car.

"Straight to your daddy," Ness said as Scott appeared in the doorway. She watched her son trot to the front door, giving Sabrina time to pull herself together. "Do you want to go for a walk?" Ness asked.

Sabrina sniffed, then opened the glove compartment to search for a napkin. Finding one, she nodded. This was familiar territory. How many times had she leaned on Ness, asked for advice and sometimes cried her eyes out over something as silly as coming in second in a gymnastic competition.

When they came to the end of the gravel driveway, they walked to the road and continued on it. Sidewalks had yet to be added to such a brand new subdivision. They walked side by side in silence, arriving at the entrance of the subdivision, where a huge gateway stood, a welcome sentinel to the new residences. Sabrina stopped there and leaned against the wall, the rough texture of the stucco barely registering. She was upset about John but had half expected him to back away. There was more to this sadness that had suddenly overcome her.

"Have you cried yet?"

"What do you mean?" Sabrina's tears had dried up the instant that sweet little boy had kissed her and told her not to cry.

"I cried like I lost my soul, with Scott, with my mom and Monica, my other sisters over the phone. I even cried with a complete stranger one day in a furniture store. I was walking through an area where televisions lined three walls. A news reporter announced that they were shooting at police officers. I was terrified for my brother Randy, his partner Frank, and at least a dozen other police officers I knew personally. Fear ran right through me. I heard a gasp and I must have made a sound because suddenly I was face to face with a woman with tears flowing down her face. She said to me, 'My husband is a police officer down there.' "

" 'So is my brother,' " I told her. Next thing I knew we had wrapped our arms around each other and were crying our eyes out. We stared at the screen a few minutes more. She thanked me and walked away. I think I texted Randy ten times that day."

"I know you were all worried about him. I was with John when he realized that Randy had had to stay."

"He's doing fine now. He's living on a cruise ship because his house was flooded. He's dealing with the memory of hearing fellow officers calling on their radios for help but drowning in their attics because they couldn't get out and no one could get to them. As for us, Scott and Devin are buying two more houses in the subdivison. They're nearly finished. Scott and I will move into one and Monica and Devin the other. My mom and dad, and Randy and his family will stay in the one we're living in now. He'll drive back and forth to work. It's better than staying on the ship, and he needs time away from the city right now."

"You guys are—"

"Lucky, I know. Both Scott and Devin have money to help make our situations better. They're working on a plan to try to help others who aren't as fortunate."

"That's good to hear."

"But we didn't walk out here to talk about Randy or Scott or Devin, or any of my family."

"Maybe one member."

"John."

"Yes, John."

"You still have a crush on him," she stated, having no need to ask.

"No, it's more. A whole lot more. I'm in love with your brother. I've pretty much told him how I feel about him and I've thrown myself at him."

"You have?"

"A couple of times."

"And what happened."

"Rejection. Rejection, again. Success, and I'm thinking that rejection is just around the corner."

"I'm sorry, Sabrina."

"I'm not surprised. John is noble and cautious and . . ."

"And not ready."

"Far from ready, so I figure I'll just have to let him go."

"Good for you."

They were quiet for a while. A soft breeze blew, sending dust swirling around their feet. "Sabrina, I'll ask again. Have you cried yet?"

"For John?"

"For John, for our city, for the people who suffered and are gone, for the streets we've walked that are now covered with filthy water. For the levees, for the inability to enter our homes to even see the damage, for the things we will never be able to salvage. For everything," she finally ended, her face scrounged up with her intensity to get it all out.

"No," Sabrina said as tears pooled at the corners of her eyes and slowly began running down her face. Hearing Ness pull it all out that way made Sabrina realize where the sadness she was feeling was coming from. It wasn't just about John. It was about everything. The tears came down faster and harder. Ness pulled her into her arms. Sabrina had stared at the television screen in shock. She had been sheltered and lived through the sounds of pounding rain and forceful wind. She'd stood in long lines waiting for prescriptions to be filled for medication that had been left at home because Grammy thought she'd be returning in a day or two. She had stood in line for unemployment, waited for hours to arrange to have Grammy's social security redirected. Waited in lines to access bank accounts, waited on hold with the insurance agency, FEMA, and the Red Cross. There had even been lines to apply for a job. Every part of her life had changed in an instant, it seemed. But if John had come to her, he would have been her silver lining in the dark, dark cloud of Katrina. Now she would have to find her own silver lining.

Sabrina hiccupped and backed away from Ness, using the napkin to dry her eyes and blow her nose. "Thanks, Ness. You were always a good shoulder to cry on."

"Hey, what are neighbors for?"

Sabrina walked back to the house with Ness, feeling lighter. Grammy had said that she was strong, and Sabrina knew that it was true. She would survive the mess Katrina had left behind and she would survive John's rejection, yet again. If he wanted something between them, then he'd have to work to get it.

"Where have the two of you been?" Mr. Calvin threw at them from just inside the front door. "We've been holding dinner for you. Look at these kids. They're nearly skin and bone!" he declared, pointed to the little ones, who were attacking a plate of crackers sitting in the middle of the coffee table as if they were starving.

"Pay no attention to him. Dinner's just ready. I've made John's favorite, stuffed bell peppers and baked macaroni. The babies needed a little something to tide them over."

"They are not babies, Maw-Maw Joyce," Vicki began.

"Oh, I forgot the pralines," Sabrina muttered as she got to the door.

"Go get 'em. I'll save you a seat next to me if you sneak me one before dinner."

"I don't know, Mr. Calvin."

"There will be no pralines before dinner. You have to set an example for the kids, Calvin."

"You're exactly right, Joycie," he said, giving Sabrina a wink.

Sabrina decided to wait until after dinner to get the pralines. Then she wouldn't get herself, or Mr. Calvin, in trouble.

The meal was a happy, messy ordeal. It couldn't have been anything else with five toddlers at the table and five kids eleven and under.

After dinner the kids begged to try on their Halloween costumes. The older kids ran upstairs to change, and the triplets and twins of course wanted to do exactly what the older kids were doing. Monica and Ness dressed them in the white ghost costumes made from pillowcases and the little ones began the Halloween fashion show.

"Five little ghosts. No variety?" Calvin commented.

"Five little ghosts for sanity's sake. You can see white in the dark. They'll literally glow and we'll know exactly where they are if they try to get away."

Next appeared a cheerleader, a ballerina, and two gory vampires who immediately chased the cheerleader and ballerina around the room.

"Where's Vicki?"

"Oh!" the girls shrieked at the same time. A second later they shouted, "Here comes the bride! Dum-dum-dum-dum."

Vicki came down the steps a second later wearing a costume version of a wedding dress. She walked right up to John and asked, "Will you marry me, Uncle John?"

"But of course," John answered, picking her up and twirling her around before handing her to Scott.

"It never fails. Vicki's been asking John to marry her each time she sees him. Talk about a crush," Ness said to her.

"At least she's getting a satisfactory answer. Maybe I should get some tips from Vicki."

"The only tip you need is to lay low. I think the timing's all wrong. Katrina's got us all unsettled. John hasn't figured out how to center himself yet."

"Neither have I," Sabrina whispered, realizing that John's rejection might be what both of them needed.

"You know, none of us Lewises have taken an easy path to love. I almost let a bigot keep me and Scott apart, and that same bigot became a member of our family about a year ago."

Sabrina followed Ness's eyes to Scott, who was rolling across the floor with his sons and nephews. Sabrina remembered when Scott had first started coming around, a widower with two little girls. He was obviously so in love with Ness that Sabrina saw it right away, realizing that race was no issue when true love was at stake.

"As for Monica and Devin, Monica was still in love with her dead husband when she met Devin. She almost allowed her love for a man, long dead and buried, to stand in the way of finding love again. Yeah," Ness sighed, "We Lewises are a bit hardheaded. I won't even get into my cousin Daniel's issues."

Sabrina laughed at the face Ness made.

"If you two were meant to be, it'll happen."

"I'm not going to hold my breath," Sabrina said, but a small tinge of hope sparked in her heart.

"I could sure use the taste of something sweet right about now." Calvin's voice reached Sabrina from across the room. "Maybe some homemade pralines," Calvin hinted.

"Sure thing, Mr. Calvin." Sabrina grinned at him and dashed to the car parked in the driveway. She pulled the pralines from under the seat and almost rammed into John, who had been standing behind her.

"Where did you go earlier?

"For a walk with Ness. We had a lot to catch up on."

"Oh, good. You do look more relaxed."

"Thank you. Your sister's good for me."

"She's good, period."

"Your entire family is, I think."

"Thank you."

"I believe I've fallen in love with them."

"You have?"

"Yeah, but I've always had a soft spot for them."

"I knew that already. Maybe too much?"

"What?"

"Forget I said that. It was just a foolish thought buzzing around in my head."

"Sure." She readily agreed, not sure she wanted to know what he was thinking.

"How about me?"

"What about you?"

"Do you have a soft spot for me?"

"Yes."

"Sabrina, we've got to talk."

"About you changing your mind and wanting to step away from me instead of with me? I know."

"How?"

"It's written all over you, John. I know you quite well."

"It's for the best. You're so young, and I feel as if I'm robbing the cradle."

"Don't explain. Live your life and I'll live mine. Sometime in the future if we're both free, then maybe we'll take that step together."

"Are you sure?"

"I'm positive."

"I don't want to hurt your feelings. I feel that I gave you an impression last night that I'm not going to be able to follow through on."

"John, I'm okay. I'm a big girl. I can handle it."

"It's just that I'll be gone and trying to have a relationship right now—"

"Where are you going?"

"James was able to make arrangements to extend our tour beyond Louisiana. We'll be visiting shelters and other cities where evacuees have relocated. We'll be going to Houston, and somewhere in Utah, then even Chicago and New York. "

"Sounds like your career is taking off."

"Exactly, which is why we're not a good thing right now. I'll be gone through Thanksgiving. I'll definitely be back by Christmas. Then maybe we can talk."

"Sure, let me get these pralines to your dad."

Sabrina headed back to the house with John walking beside her, trying not to put too much stock into his words. He'd never liked hurting her feelings. He had always taken up for her when Josh, his twin, had teased her. If pity was all he had to offer, then she didn't want any of it. It was all or nothing, Sabrina had already decided, and if she had to wait for all, she'd do it on her own terms.

CHAPTER 8

A long bus ride left a lot of time for thinking, and John was doing a great deal of it.

All of his thoughts were centered on Sabrina.

The image of her as a kid had been completely shattered. It had all begun with that kiss in Mississippi. Shock had made him literally push her away despite the arousal he felt at the touch of her lips and press of her soft body against him. His own confusion had caused him to be as harsh as Josh had always been to her. He had regretted it immediately, but he hadn't wanted her to see that.

Somehow she had.

Sabrina claimed she knew him and now John was positive that she did, better than he knew himself, it seemed. When had she grown into such an intuitive, strong woman? A woman he was running away from because he felt as if she fit like a specially designed fixture in every aspect of his life, except his music.

He needed his music.

He needed to be free to express himself, to stretch his talent and see where it would take him. He needed to be unencumbered, unattached. He had done the sensible thing and gone straight to college instead of diving into the music world. He'd majored in music education and had even taken a job teaching music at a local junior high that centered on the arts so that he would have a steady income. He had done that for three years, while playing as a backup and sometimes replacement trumpet player for any jazz band he could land a spot with. And his big break had come with his first real gig at the casino in Mississippi. And then Sabrina came along. When Katrina blew in, the hurricane pulled them together even tighter. John hadn't realized exactly how much she had gotten under his skin until he saw her kissing James. John had never been a violent person, but he had wanted to do some serious violence to James that day. And after that, to shake some sense into her. Instead, she shook all sense out of him. God, he'd never been so confused in his life.

"One focus, one thing at a time," he muttered to himself.

"You say something, Red?" James asked.

"Not a thing," John answered. The intro bars of the first selection they would be playing ran through his head as he shifted his focus to his music, getting lost in the melody playing inside his head.

"You're not thinking about that girl of yours, are you?"

No, John almost said, then thought better of it. If James thought Sabrina was free, then he'd be after her like white on rice. "Yeah, she's on my mind."

"Damn straight she'd better be. The minute she's off yours she'll be on mine."

"I'll remember that," John told him, the music in his head fading as Sabrina moved to the forefront again. He pictured her with his family. She had blended right in, with his sisters, mom and dad, and of course the kids. Yet somehow he found himself at odds about Sabrina and his family. He was pleased that she fit in so well but wondered if her feelings for him were all tied up with how she felt about his family. It was a fleeting and ridiculous thought that he had almost given voice to. Good thing he'd learned at an early age when to keep his mouth shut. She loved his family and they loved her, case closed. And an announcement that they were a couple would have been a welcome surprise. She had expected such an announcement that day in Gonzales, but he had not been able to declare when it came right down to it. He still felt guilty about that. Maybe a declaration would be forthcoming someday, if she would still have him sometime in the future, but not now. He'd surprise her. Which probably wouldn't be so much a surprise to Ness and his mom.

"Think about what it is you really want in life, little brother," Ness had advised before he had gotten into the car that evening.

His mom, who saw everything, had handed him a plate to take with him. When he had opened it to warm the next day there was a little note inside. *Do what's important to you. I'm proud of who you are.*

His dad had simply told him, "Play from your heart and be back here for Christmas!"

John felt as if he was following their advice, yet a small part of him didn't agree.

Sabrina.

Later. He would deal with her later, he assured himself.

Of course a short time *later* their last moments together rolled through his head.

"So," he had said as they stood in front of her Uncle Darren's house after a silent drive from Gonzales.

"So," she repeated. "I guess this is goodbye until Christmas."

"I suppose it is," he had said, suddenly feeling depressed. He wanted to have his cake and eat it, too. Christmas was months away. A lot could happen in a few of months. It wouldn't be fair to make promises or to expect any from her but he needed contact. "I'll call you once in a while."

"Sure. Do you have still my cell phone number?"

"Yeah, you gave it to me at the shelter." And he hadn't called it once yet. The thought lay unsaid between them, but she hadn't called him either. "Do you still have mine?"

"Yes."

Craving more than a number John asked, "Can I e-mail you?"

"Sure."

These one-word answers were starting to annoy him. She was digging inside her purse for something to write on. She pulled out a half sheet of paper with a list of numbers and e-mail addresses for hurricane victims. On the back she wrote her e-mail address. Taking it from her, he felt a mixture of regret and longing. He had planned on tearing the paper in half and writing his e-mail address for her. After all, it was his suggestion, but he suddenly got cold feet. He was asking too much of her with no real commitment from him. The last thing he wanted to do was lead her on. If he didn't give her his e-mail address, then she couldn't contact him unless he made the first move. Since he was still not sure what that move would be, he forced himself to fold the piece of paper and slip it into his back pocket.

The expectation of an exchange of e-mail addresses hung in the air. John was surprised that she didn't comment on his lack of sharing. "Well, good-bye then," he told her, desperate to feel her lips, her breath, her body pressing against his own. Instead he turned away.

"John." Her fingers touched his own, a light brush that pulled at him. "Could I at least get a good-bye kiss, one to last me until I see you again?"

John didn't hesitate. He pulled her toward him, wrapping his hands around her waist. He stared at her for a full minute, taking in a face that he already knew so well but at the same time was new to him. Her expressive eyes, her smooth brown skin, her nose that plumbed out at the side but narrowed at the tip, that lopsided grin that let him know that he was being ridiculous again. Ah, but it didn't feel that way.

"John."

"Yeah."

"Kiss me before Uncle Darren comes home and threatens to shoot you with his gun."

"Uncle Darren's here and he thinks a little air between the two of you might be a good idea," her uncle said, coming up the steps, moving past them before going inside. "Stay out here too long and I'm going to have to come back out to hose the two of you down, and after that I might shoot," he said before closing the door.

At the sound of her uncle's voice Sabrina *had* moved to allow a bit of air between them. She closed the gap the moment the door closed and tilted her head up toward his chin where she pressed soft kisses. John took her mouth, pulling her even closer, his hands moving down to her bottom, which he lightly caressed. The kiss deepened, driving him to pull her even closer. Her soft breasts pressed against his chest, and his hardness was level with her pelvis, his hands capturing her rear to hold her against him. He kissed her until he felt as if he couldn't breathe. He pulled back, taking deep even breaths, her head resting against his shoulder. As oxygen entered his brain he recalled that her uncle was as good as his word and would probably be out here to toss a bucket of water on them. John forced his hand to move up. Caressing her shoulders, he gently pulled away from her. He felt as if everything she had wanted to say was in that kiss. He didn't want to know, or think, about what she wanted from him. No promises, he reminded himself.

"Until Christmas."

"Christmas," she said, before going into the house.

"Christmas," John whispered, staring at the monotonous scenery of cattle and fields as they made their way to Houston. He dug into his bag and pulled out some sheet music. If he was going to think about Sabrina, he might as well put thought to music. A song began pouring from his soul and onto paper, giving him some degree of peace and some hope that maybe he could merge Sabrina and his music together.

Exactly two weeks after saying good-bye to John and a week before Halloween, Sabrina finally got a job. She was hired as a physical education teacher at an elementary school that been reopened because the local school district had acquired over three hundred more students, thanks to Hurricane Katrina. The job title was not quite her line of work but close enough. Sabrina figured that she could easily incorporate dance into the curriculum. Dance was, after all, a form of aerobic exercise. She was also offered a position as a dance teacher for the after school program, which she jumped at. She had been given a quick tour and now stood in the middle of the gym that would essentially be her classroom. It was on the small side for a gym but definitely big enough to dance across and play sports. Sabrina made her way across the shiny wooden floor, entering a small room that the principal had pointed out as Sabrina's office before dashing off to some emergency. The room had a teacher's desk and four or five student desks, but not much else. She would definitely need to get a few supplies and clean things up a bit. Facing the gym again, she thought of adding a few Halloween decorations and beginning her first week with a round of exercises centered on the upcoming holiday. A mummy relay and apple toss would be a fun way to teach team effort. Her first dance for her after-school group could be based on the song "The Monster Mash." Ideas began rushing through her head so fast that she barely registered that her phone was ringing.

"Hey, Ness," she said, having recognized the number.

"Well?" she asked.

"I've got a job and I start on Monday!"

"Great, I knew you'd land one of those jobs you'd applied for. We'll have to celebrate. Are you still coming over this weekend?"

"Of course. I'll need to stop by my Uncle Darren's house to pick up Grammy and we'll be on our way. See you soon." Sabrina clicked her cell phone closed and did a twirling spin across the entire gym.

"I'm happy to see that you're full of so much enthusiasm," the principal said behind her.

Sabrina straightened, attempting to look and act like a teacher. "I'm excited. I can't wait to get started."

"These students will need a teacher with that attitude and energy. Welcome, Miss Adams."

"Thank you," Sabrina said, making her way back to the front of the school, feeling even more excited if that were possible.

Before she could make it to her car, her cell phone rang again. It was Ness.

"Sorry to call back so soon, but Dad wanted to know if Grammy had made any more pralines."

"Tell him I can't promise him anything, but I'll see."

Sabrina laughed as she hung up the phone. She had offered to join Ness, Monica, Miss Joyce and Mr. Calvin with their volunteer efforts. They alternated helping at shelters and distribution centers for evacuees of Hurricane Katrina and Rita. Two of them would stay with the kids while the other two spent a few hours offering what help they could. Grammy was dying to see the Lewises again and Sabrina had jumped at the chance to have something to do, not to mention an open door to John and what he'd been up to. Sabrina didn't have a clue to how things were working out for him. He hadn't called or e-mailed.

Not once.

She still couldn't believe that she had let him get away without getting *his* e-mail address. But she had intentionally left the ball in his court. Of course getting information wasn't the only reason she had arranged the visit. Now that she had gotten help from FEMA, a partial insurance payment and all things Grammy under wraps, sitting around the house had begun to grow old. Grammy was back to her old self and didn't need constant supervision, and Uncle Darren's work hours had finally stabilized. Sabrina needed something to do. Reacquainting herself with the Lewises and helping others who were not as lucky as she and Grammy seemed like the thing to do. So what if she got a little insight into what was happening with John in the process? It's not as if she were obsessing about him. If anyone had been obsessing, it was Grammy. Having no real answers to give her as to why she and John weren't "together," Sabrina had steadily steered her toward focusing on Darren and Diane. Not that Grammy had forgotten about her and

John; she was just more focused on the two who were close at hand.

"Grammy!" Sabrina called, walking into the house forty-five minutes later from a ride that should have taken ten minutes. The congestion caused by after-school traffic and the additional temporary residents of Lafayette had not diminished her good mood.

"Grammy, dear! Where are you?" Sabrina called, sprinting into the kitchen.

" 'Grammy, dear'? You're in a good mood." Grammy took a pan of brownies out of the oven. "I'm suspecting that I'm getting my old Sabrina back now that you've gotten a teaching job."

"Then you're suspecting right."

"Have you heard from John?" Grammy turned to close the oven door.

"No to that. But I'm excited about visiting the Lewises again."

"I'll betcha they've heard from John. You could get some answers from them as to why he's gone mum."

Although Grammy had expressed what Sabrina herself had been planning to do, in a tactful way of course, worry ran through her. "Grammy, I will do no such thing and neither will you."

"Oh, all right."

"I mean it." Sabrina paused. "Did you say all right?"

"Yes, I said all right, but only because I'm not going."

"What do you mean, you're not going?" Sabrina asked as the house phone rang and Grammy moved like a teenager, catching it on the second ring.

"Is that you, Faith?" A long pause. "Everything's ready, then?" Grammy asked, a gleeful expression taking over her face. "You do your part and I'll do mine," she said mysteriously, replacing the phone with a cheerful smirk.

"What are you up to, Grammy?"

"Making two people see sense."

"Uncle Darren and Diane?"

"Of course. That's why I can't go with you to see the Lewises. Give them my apologies."

"Sure, but what's up?"

Sabrina didn't have to ask twice. Grammy was beside herself with excitement about her plans. "Faith and I have cooked up a scheme to get the two of them together for longer than two seconds. We've done some investigating and have figured out that they had something going on before Faith came to live with Diane because of that hip surgery. But these foolish folks had a falling out. We're working to get them back together."

Pleased that Grammy's and Miss Faith's attentions were focused far from her, Sabrina grilled her for details. "What do you plan to do?"

"Faith's going to get herself stuck in the bathroom. The lock's been acting funny, so Diane won't expect that something fishy is going on."

"Why has the lock been acting funny?"

"Don't worry about that. Diane's been meaning to fix it but hasn't had the time to see about it. I suggested that she ask your Uncle Darren but her face gets all stiff whenever I say his name so I knew she wouldn't ask."

"So you're taking it a step farther."

"I have to. Diane's a stubborn one," Grammy said, finding a butter knife and cutting the brownies into squares. "Well, anyway, Faith's going to really get stuck, so stuck Diane won't be able to open the door."

"And then she'll have to ask for help."

"And being such a nervous thing where Faith is concerned, who else would she ask but her next door neighbor?"

"Who else?"

"No one else."

"Then what?"

"Darren will fix the problem. He's as good with his hands as his daddy was." A dreamy expression appeared on Grammy's face and Sabrina didn't want to figure out what that meant.

"And then what? How will getting Uncle Darren to rescue Miss Faith get the two of them together?"

"There's more to the plan if you just listen, smarty pants," Grammy said, transferring the warm brownies to a plastic container.

"Then tell me."

"I'll insist that Darren show Diane what the problem is so it won't happen again. And even though she won't want to get near him she'll do it because she'll do anything to make sure Faith is safe."

"How devious."

"Do you want to hear the rest of this?"

"Of course."

"Then hush and listen. Faith's going to ask for her walker. She'll leave it in the bathroom. She doesn't need that thing anymore anyway. I'll tell Darren to get me a towel or something and then when they're inside we're going to slam the door shut and lock it from the outside."

"How?"

"Faith and I installed one of those hook and screw locks at the top of the door. They'll be so worried about the one on the knob that they'll never see it."

"Grammy!"

"What? It's for their own good."

"I'm glad I'm not going to be here. How long are you going to keep them in there?"

"A good hour, I think."

"And what do you expect to happen in an hour?"

"Maybe some real talking."

"Neither one of them will be too happy with either one of you."

"They'll get over it. We're two little old ladies with nothing to do. We'll be easily forgiven, just wait and see. You go on and get yourself out of here. Darren's off work today but he said he'd be home for dinner and I'm softening him up with one of his favorites."

"Shrimp stew?"

"You guessed it. Now here." Thrusting the plastic container full of brownies at her, Grammy busied herself around the kitchen, so much like her old self Sabrina had to grin. "Take those with you. Tell Calvin I made them especially for him."

Sabrina laughed. "He was looking for pralines."

"That'll have to do," she said, pulling a large pot out of one of the kitchen cabinets.

"They will. Do you want me to stay and help?"

"No, I want you to go and visit with your future in-laws and find out why you haven't heard a peep from John."

"Grammy!"

"I can't have you hanging around here. You might accidentally sabotage all our plans. So get out of here. I'll deal with you and John later."

"But you promised to stay out of my business with John."

"That promise was made under stress. Go on, get going, I have less than two hours to get this dinner done."

Backing out of the kitchen, Sabrina went into her room to quickly change into jeans and a T-shirt and to grab her overnight bag. If Grammy ever focused that much thought and attention on her and John, they were in for it. Sabrina hoped that they would come to some kind of understanding before Grammy and Miss Faith got involved.

CHAPTER 9

"To be a pest, or not to be a pest, that is the question," Sabrina said aloud on her drive to Gonzales, debating whether or not she should call John.

After dinner with the Lewises, an impromptu dance session with the girls, a rousing coloring fiasco with five "little, big kids," as they'd been dubbed by Vicki, the thought remained in the back of her mind until miraculously the house became quiet.

"Ah, the stroke of eight," Mr. Calvin said, joining Sabrina in the den.

"What does that mean?" Sabrina asked.

"The older kids are taking baths and the little, big kids are being put to bed," Miss Joyce said, bringing in a tray with coffee.

"And their parents are doing the putting," her husband added.

"Something you enjoy doing yourself."

"But only when I want to, Joycie. I never *have* to. It's the joy of being a grandpa. I never *have* to do anything"

"Well, I never met a man who *wanted* to more than you."

A patter of little feet announced the arrival of one of Monica's boys, who darted to his grandfather, a book in hand. "Read to me, Paw-Paw, please, read."

"And it just so happens, I feel like reading to a little boy named," his grandfather stooped to make a face as he stared at him long and hard, "Chance!" he finally said.

"I'm Aaron! You know I'm Aaron!" The little voice trailed away as his grandfather carried him up the stairs.

"Monica! Devin! You lost one!" Mr. Calvin bellowed at the top of the stairs.

Sabrina smiled. This visit was making her fall in love with the Lewises all over again.

"Help yourself to coffee," Miss Joyce offered, sitting back before asking, "Have you heard from—"

"Maw-Maw Joyce! Telephone!" saved Sabrina from having to answer that particular question. A dripping wet Megan, with a towel carelessly wrapped around her, came from the back of the house, clenching a cordless receiver.

"Megan!" her grandmother began in admonishment.

"It's Uncle John!" Megan announced. Sabrina could tell by the look on her little face that she was hoping to save herself from a whole lot of trouble with that bit of information.

"Oh!" Miss Joyce took the wet phone from Megan. From the surprised excitement in her voice it seemed as if she hadn't talked to John since he left. That bit of news gave Sabrina a feeling of relief. If he hadn't had enough time to talk to his family, it would explain why she hadn't heard from him either.

"You'd better run up and dry off before you do get into trouble," Sabrina advised the still dripping little girl who was now intent on hearing her grandmother's side of the conversation.

"Good idea," she said, running to the back of the house where she had come from earlier.

The news traveled quickly. Soon the den was full again, minus the little, big kids who, it seemed, when put down for the night, stayed down for the night. The phone passed from adult to adult and finally to each of the older kids, who were now all dry and pajama clad.

"Here you go, Sabrina," seven-year-old Mark said, handing her the phone.

Sabrina froze, not knowing how to react. She hadn't expected to have the opportunity to talk to John. He'd called his family, not her.

"It's your turn," he explained, waving the phone in his hand.

"You can go in the living room if you'd like a little privacy," Ness suggested. "This room is about to be taken over by Movie Night."

"Yes, take the call in the living room. It's going to be too noisy in here in a minute," Miss Joyce agreed.

As if that decided it, Mark placed the phone into her lap. Sabrina could hear John's voice. "Hello, anybody there?"

What was the matter with her? Of course she wanted to talk to him, and this way the ball wasn't in anyone's court. It just happened. She stood, putting the phone to her ear as she walked toward the living room. Still, she heard the attempt of John's dad at whispering.

"What was that all about?"

"I'll tell you later, Calvin," was the reply.

"Hello," Sabrina said as she entered the dimly lit room.

"Finally a person." John's deep, gentle voice was a pleasure to hear. "I didn't want to hang up because of that time about a week after the storm when I hung up on my end and Vicki left the phone off the hook. I couldn't contact you guys for hours and I was already a nervous wreck. I didn't want the line tied up again."

"I understand," Sabrina said, purposely not telling him who he was talking to. Would he recognize her voice? She wanted him to recognize her voice.

"This isn't Ness or Monica, is it?"

"No, neither one."

"Sabrina," he said with a longing that she hadn't thought she'd ever hear. "What are you doing there?"

"Visiting."

"Oh, I'm—"

"Don't apologize."

"How do you know I was going to apologize?"

"I know you, John, remember?" She laughed because she could picture the look of confusion on his face.

"I remember. I'm not used to it, but I remember."

"I'm not upset that you haven't called or e-mailed. I didn't expect you to. I'm not chasing after you, John."

"Good, I don't want you to."

"But," she added, letting the word hang between them.

"But what?"

"If you were doing the chasing I'd let myself be caught." Sabrina couldn't believe she was saying this to him. She knew she would not have said these words to anyone else. With John they felt right. It was the same as following him to the casino because she knew what she wanted. This was a bit direct, but still more subtle than throwing herself at him that night.

"Okay, that's good to know."

"So, if you want to talk once in awhile I'm here."

"Actually, I've wanted to call."

"You have?" Sabrina's heart started to pound. The hand that gripped the phone was probably as damp as Megan's was when she'd handed the phone to her grandmother earlier.

"I've been thinking about you."

"You have?"

"Nonstop."

"Which means?"

"I can't get you out of my mind, so I might as well enjoy having you there."

"What other option is there?"

"I could torment myself by trying to keep you out of mind but it only leads me to imagining you with some other guy."

"Are you trying to compliment or insult me?"

"I didn't mean to do either."

"I know. You don't have a malicious bone in your body."

"Aw, 'Brina, you do know me. How about we begin this thing between us all over again? Let's start by talking."

"We already are."

"I meant really talking. Can I call you later? We're about to go on stage in a few minutes."

"Of course."

"Then bye, for now anyway."

"Until later."

"Later," he repeated.

"Red, you really *played* that trumpet tonight," James slapped him on his back as he caught up with John. "What happened to you? Did you get some spiritual uplifting or something?" he asked just before a fan stopped them for autographs.

Pausing to think, as he autographed a napkin with the logo of the club where they were playing, John realized that tonight was the first time he had allowed his music to take over him. He had always been in control before, but tonight the music had controlled him. John smiled as he handed the napkin back to the middle-aged woman who had complimented the band, related her Katrina story and the comfort she got from hearing them play. This was a regular occurrence, making him feel as if he were doing something to help people cope. It was these kinds of interactions that had him re-thinking his decision to leave Sabrina alone. That and the fact that he couldn't get her out of his mind.

Every Katrina story pricked his heart, especially those he heard at shelters. There were those who'd struggled to evacuate before the storm with barely enough money to pay for gas, and those who'd piled in cars with neighbors and relatives. Then, more and more, he began to meet those who didn't, or couldn't, evacuate. People without transportation and those who had thought Katrina would go the way that Ivan had the year before and they'd be hours on the road for no apparent reason. He had gotten some firsthand accounts of experiences at the Superdome and Convention Center and on roof tops that went straight to his heart. There were people who had watched family members dying without being able to do anything to help. They all shared the misery of Katrina but they were also comforted by the music. They had lost so much, but simply bringing a piece of home to their shattered lives was a balm to their spirits. It made John think of Sabrina and the comforting presence she had been for him during the storm and directly after. She had said he was there for her but she had kept him grounded. With so much of his life still up in the air, why was he running away from someone who made him feel so alive?

A thought eased into his mind, bringing him to a realization. "Hey," John called, getting James's attention. "I was lifted, but not by any spirits." Sabrina and their brief exchange had opened him up to a side of himself he hadn't known existed. It was like a deep awakening that had enhanced his music. Thinking about Sabrina and opening up to the possibility of what they could have had sent the music soaring through his veins. He should have recognized it the moment they connected, but he had been too busy seeing Sabrina the teenager. That image had completely overshadowed Sabrina the woman. Tonight his music had flowed with an intensity and freedom he had never experienced before.

It was all because of Sabrina.

Sabrina was his, and he wanted her.

And it was perfectly normal to want her in his life. She was a part of his music. No, she was the chord that had been missing from his music.

John needed to talk to her, tell her what he was feeling. Glancing at his watch he saw that it was midnight. It was too late to call today. When he had said he would call later, had she expected him to call tonight? John didn't think so.

Tomorrow, he'd call first thing in the morning.

As soon as he got to his hotel room he showered and plopped onto the bed.

Sleep wouldn't come.

The same emotions that had driven him to pull her into his arms for the first time were coursing through him with ten times the intensity. He wasn't going to sleep tonight. His mind was working overtime, sending a message to his body, translating it into a need that was beginning to overwhelm him.

Oh, but he more than needed Sabrina. John craved her: her touch, her grin, that say-anything mouth of hers.

The numbers on the clock flashed red at him. One o'clock. It was even later and his craving had only increased. It was as if finally accepting her in his life had torn down the barrier he had been trying to maintain.

Hopping out of bed, he went down to the lobby and sat at one of the computers available for guests. He logged on to his e-mail service and clicked the icon to write a message. He stared at the screen.

What could he say? Well, he could say that he missed her.

Sabrina, I miss you.

John looked at the words he had typed. It was the truth, but so blah. Deleting that line, he thought a minute, then began typing again.

Sabrina, I'm hoping later is much sooner than we think.

Then he added something more.

Missing you,

John

Not all he wanted to say, but so much more than nothing. He clicked the send button and closed his account.

Much too soon he was lying in the middle of the bed again. He felt as if he had accomplished *something*, but it was just that it seemed about as effective as feeding a crumb to a starving man. He was that starving man. It was self-inflicted starvation but starvation all the same.

Her voice.

He had to at least hear her voice.

Determined to have that much, John reached for his cell phone, flipped it open, and knowing the number by heart, began to dial. Earlier, when he had told her that he had wanted to call, he hadn't been making it up as some kind of excuse. Every night since he had left, he had pulled up her number from his address book and stared at it before deciding that it was a bad idea to call.

"Hello," he heard before his fingers hit the keypad.

"Sabrina," he said, putting the phone to his ear, immediately recognizing her voice.

"Yes, it's me. I was online. I got your e-mail, and I thought that since we were both awake that I'd call, so that's what I did."

"I'm glad you did. I was about to call you."

"No wonder I didn't hear the phone ring. You must have picked it up at the exact moment that I dialed." Sabrina cringed, feeling unsure of herself where John was concerned.

No, it didn't ring. Are you okay?"

"Yes. No, I'm just nervous. I ramble when I'm nervous."

"What's making you nervous?"

"You."

"Me?"

"Yes, and I can't explain why. I've never been nervous with you before."

"That's definitely true."

"And I ramble when I'm nervous."

"I've noticed."

"I think I'm going to stop talking for awhile."

"Please don't. I called for the exact purpose of hearing your voice."

"Oh."

"So," John asked when Sabrina's end of the phone went silent, "are we going to breathe on the phone for a while?"

Sabrina laughed, feeling the tension ease out of her. After all, this was John.

"No. I thought your e-mail was very sweet."

"I'm glad you think so."

"And romantic."

"I was shooting for direct and to the point, but if it came out as romantic then it was because of you."

"Because of me?"

"You've been on my mind since Mississippi."

"Ah, 'The Mississippi Incident.' " Sabrina said, beginning to relax even more. Yes, this was her John. He had always been her John. He was just realizing it and the change, even though it was exactly what she had craved, had thrown her for a minute. Actually, it was the e-mail that had thrown her. It was his first real attempt at confirming his feelings for her, and it had made her nervous.

"Is that what we're calling it?"

"It's better than calling it 'Scaring John-Half-Out-of-His-Wits.' "

"You're right."

"Which led us to 'The Katrina Incident.' "

"There's that, too."

"Have I thanked you for being there for me, John?"

"Not with words."

"Well, here they are. Thank you for being my shelter in the storm."

" 'Brina, you didn't need me. You were a shelter for every person in there. I think that was when I began to realize that you weren't a kid anymore."

"And that scared you."

"Mmmm," he answered, ashamed of the way he had acted. "Not anymore."

"Where does that lead us now?"

"Past 'The Dinner Incident' and the 'The Trip to Gonzales Incident.' "

"We've been through a lot of incidents." Sabrina laughed and John could just picture the lopsided grin taking over her face.

"I wish I was there with you."

"Why?"

"To kiss that grin off your face."

"I'd enjoy that."

"And after that?"

"I'd let you catch me in your arms."

"And I'd keep you there, for a very, very long time."

"John." Sabrina paused. This conversation was so close to the kind she had wished for that she started to get nervous for a whole other reason. "John, you're not lying to me, are you? If you're telling me all this because you're hundreds of miles away and you feel that it's safe to give me false hope because you're so far away then—"

" 'Brina, you're rambling."

"—I'd have to tell you—"

" 'Brina! No!"

"What?"

"I said, no, I'm not just telling you these things because I'm so far away. Sabrina, you're like music to me."

"What?"

"It took me awhile to see it, but tonight, after staying away from you for so long just talking to you made me feel it."

"Like music?"

"Yes."

"Do you know what you're saying?"

"That I'm not going to try to run away. I want to see you. We'll be leaving Texas and heading to Chicago and a few other places in between before making our way back to Louisiana to do some gigs at a few local schools. Can you meet me somewhere in between?"

"I've got a job. I'm a physical education teacher at a school in Lafayette. I start on Monday."

"That's great and lousy at the same time."

"I know."

"I knew you'd find a job. You're great with kids."

"You picked that up from the whole week we taught together?"

"That's all it takes, and from watching you with my nieces and nephews, it's a given. Why were you there tonight?"

"I'm still there. I came to visit your family."

"Oh," he said, adding nothing to the short, satisfied-sounding syllable.

"Oh?"

"I think I like that. You and my family."

"You do?"

"As long as it's more me than my family that you're falling for. I don't want to sound conceited but I'm the number one Lewis in your life, right?" he asked with a degree of uncertainty Sabrina was surprised to hear.

"Of course."

"Then yes." John let the doubt he had been periodically feeling slide to the back of his head. "I'll say it again, you and my family, I like that."

"What I'd like is to see you."

"You will. I'll find a way to make it happen," John promised, determined to make it up to her. If he hadn't been so hardheaded they would have had some time to spend together. He could have easily made it back a couple of days between gigs when they still were playing at shelters in Louisiana. "Was that a yawn?"

"No." A huge, breathy pause filled the phone.

"That's why I wasn't going to call. It's gotten really late."

"It's only three o'clock."

"And within a couple of hours you'll be rudely awakened by a mob of children."

"Probably."

"I'll call you tomorrow."

"Promise?"

"I'll catch you then," John said, hearing the soft laugh on the other end of the phone showing him that she understood the earlier reference to her promise to allow herself to be caught if he were doing the chasing. "Good night."

"Good night," she answered.

John flipped his cell phone closed, his eyes following suit as he pictured the grin on her face and imagined himself doing something very satisfying to make it disappear.

CHAPTER 10

By the middle of the day Sabrina had spoken to John two times.

For about two minutes before he went to rehearsal, which he was late for because he had overslept.

Then for about thirty seconds before a woman, who looked to be about eighty years old, shuffled toward her and asked for help in finding a pair of slippers. Feeling a bit put out because she had been waiting hours for his phone call, Sabrina said a quick goodbye with a promise to call him back.

The old woman went on to explain how she needed a new pair of slippers because the ones she was wearing had a hole and all of her other shoes were lost in the storm.

Feeling a little ashamed of herself, Sabrina guided the woman to the donated rack of shoes at the distribution center where she had spent the day with Ness and Miss Joyce. Monica had stayed home because she had discovered, that very morning, that Jasmine had volunteered her to bake two dozen cupcakes and a pan of brownies to sell at an after-school bake sale for her soccer team.

Helping the old lady reminded Sabrina once again of just how lucky she and Grammy were. Although they hadn't had immediate access to their funds, they had had

Uncle Darren, who had supplied them with more clothes, a roof, and security.

"These are just perfect," said the woman, holding up a pair of baby blue Daniel Green slippers. "Just like the kind I used to use to paddle my children's butts when they were naughty. I had at least two pair at home, but I don't paddle my children anymore. They're grown." She sighed, her eyes watery pools. "You know," she went on, not seeming to notice or care if Sabrina was still listening, "sometimes, I can go a whole day without thinking about the things I lost, 'cause after all I'm alive. But every once in a while I remember something that's forever gone because of Katrina."

"Mama," a much younger woman called from across the spacious open area that used to be the service department of a Wal-Mart. "What are you doing way over here? We came to get food, not clothes. We got clothes last time we were here."

"It's getting better, though," the old woman said, edging closer to Sabrina to whisper. "In the beginning, I would remember something that was gone every few minutes, then every few hours."

"Mama," the woman said again, a child's hand in one of her own, the other steering a basket filled with donated food items, "we have to go. I've got an interview for an apartment in twenty minutes. Don't you want to move out of the campgrounds?"

"Now," she continued as if her daughter wasn't bearing down on them, "once a day is all I'm plagued with. I can deal with that."

"Mama!" The woman had finally reached them. "We have to go."

"I needed slippers." She held up the pair in her hands.

"Daniel Greens," the woman smiled.

Sabrina wondered what she had to smile about. What memory had they brought to mind?

"This young lady helped me find them."

"Thank you, miss," the woman said before turning to her mother. "We have to go, Mama."

"It was nothing." Sabrina's voice faded as the trio departed, leaving her feeling as if it really was nothing. The little bit she had done didn't feel like much. But having someone to sort and stack donations had to be beneficial in some way.

No longer annoyed that her phone conversation had been cut short, Sabrina spent the next hour helping others find some of the basic necessities so that they could work toward rebuilding their lives. She'd have time to build a relationship with John.

They'd have lots of time.

Time.

It seemed to fly by. Every minute of it was filled with essential tasks John could not get away from, and the most essential of all, he could not perform.

All he wanted was five minutes to spend on the phone talking to his girl.

Hours of practice and a few more spent rearranging the stage, barely gave him time to dial her number once as he shifted from practice to setup. Then she couldn't talk.

This was payback from God. "Wasn't Katrina enough?" he asked, as he hurried onto the bus to change. Rarely had he dwelt on how much he had lost. His side of a double he had rented in Mid-City had water, he was certain. The area was one that was not immediately accessible. Only specific zip codes in the city had opened and he'd been too busy trying to earn a living to even think about getting into the area to salvage anything. All he could think about today was finding some time to talk to Sabrina.

He dashed toward the rear of the bus to find his suitcase, checking his cell phone along the way. He found two missed calls, both from Sabrina. One he knew about because his hip had vibrated earlier when he was loading his luggage into the bus after they had checked out for the day. His hands hadn't been free to answer. The second one hadn't even registered.

" 'Brina," he said at her sweet hello, as he attempted to hop into his pants. "I'm dying here."

"You are?"

"Yep, I've decided that I'm being punished."

"By whom?"

"By the one and only man upstairs."

"God's punishing you?

"You better believe it."

"And what exactly are you being punished for?"

"For throwing the gift he sent me back in his face."

"What gift?"

"You," he said, spinning in a circle as he tried to get his arm through a sleeve while holding the cell phone to his ear with his shoulder. "He's making it impossible for me to do something as simple as talk to you as punishment for my stupidity," he added, succeeding in getting his other arm through the sleeve. "Are you still there?" John asked when he didn't hear a sound on the other end of the line. Losing the signal, leaving him talking to himself, would be just the thing that would happen to him right about now.

"I'm here," Sabrina answered. "I'm just not used to hearing you talk like that."

"Get used to it. I've got a feeling that I'll be talking exactly like this on a regular basis for no other reason than it feels right."

"I'll learn to deal with it."

"Good. " And even though John couldn't see her, he knew that she was wearing that lopsided grin of hers. "Now," he continued, "I'm not just calling because I miss you like crazy. I'm calling to let you know I'll be calling later, much later, after tonight's performance. I'm getting dressed now. Correction, I am dressed and have two minutes to make my way backstage." Pausing to take a breath he added, "I've been thinking about you all day."

"Me, too."

"And I believe we've got a chance to see each other. I've got a plan. I'll tell you about it later. Gotta go!"

"Bye," Sabrina said to the empty line, thrilled at the excitement she could literally feel coming through the phone. Her quiet, soft-spoken, gentle John was really letting her in. That two-minute conversation and abrupt goodbye should have frustrated her. Instead, she felt as if a window were opening into a whole new beginning for them.

Friday evening Sabrina sat in heavy traffic on Interstate 10, on her way to meet John in Baton Rouge. It seemed that every New Orleanian who had settled in cities and towns northwest of New Orleans was heading home this weekend. Some perhaps to view a destroyed home for the first time. Others maybe to begin, or to continue, repairs. She and Grammy had done neither but they had discussed options with Uncle Darren as to what should be done about the house. Those thoughts would fill her mind pretty soon, she was sure, but not today.

Sabrina was determined that they wouldn't today.

Unlike many of those sharing the highway with her, she wasn't ready to head back to New Orleans to confront the depressing scenes of the city she loved. She was on the road today making her way to man that she loved.

Oh, yes, she loved John.

Sabrina was sitting in all this traffic so that she could meet John in Baton Rouge. Most of the band members had family who had temporarily relocated there, so they were making a brief stop before continuing north, playing various gigs until they reached Chicago, then made their way back to Louisiana. They would be in Baton Rouge for three hours only.

Sabrina would have three blissful hours to spend with John, a John who was no longer in denial. Unfortunately, three hours had been reduced to two when Sabrina discovered that she had to stay an hour after school for a mandatory faculty meeting, a meeting she definitely couldn't miss, having just completed her first week of work. The hour-long informative meeting had threatened to go into overtime because of an extremely inquisitive second grade teacher who began to ask lengthy, detailed questions specific to her classroom, having *NOTHING* to do with anyone else in the room. Sabrina had felt as if she would explode. One hour had already been taken away; she would not sacrifice a minute more. Staring holes into the petite, squeaky-voiced teacher, Sabrina attempted to mentally relay the message that her mouth needed to close. The telekinetic vibes were obviously bouncing off since she noticed many of her other colleagues were giving the offending teacher similar looks. Oblivious to all, she took a deep breath and launched into another lengthy question. Sabrina shifted her mental powers to the principal, directing her to end the conversation and the meeting immediately.

"Mrs. Johnson," the principal began, "since that issue affects only you, I will be glad to discuss it after the meeting. Teachers, have a nice weekend."

"Yes!" A giant exclamation point had vibrated inside of Sabrina's head as she'd sashayed across the room, her legs taking her out of the building, into the car, and directly into traffic.

There had been Lafayette traffic due to the influx of evacuees into the city. Then there was the congestion of I-10 with so many people driving into the city now that nearly all bans for allowing people in to view their homes had been lifted.

Even though her tolerance for sitting in snail-dragging-through-molasses traffic had increased during her evacuation, the traffic was wearing on her because her time with John was being eaten away as she crawled along.

It was amazing how she viewed her current situation. There was life pre-Katrina and life post-Katrina. Pre-Katrina she would have been grumbling and moaning about the delay even if she had had no place to go or nowhere to be. She was dying to see John, but it wasn't a life or death crisis. She had been saturated with many of those via the TV screen barely two months ago, had nearly tasted a bit of that herself before being rescued off the highway the night before the storm.

Still, she did have somewhere to go and someone to go to. *And* she had to go to the bathroom.

The ringing of the phone broke through her frustrated patience.

"Where are you now?" John asked.

"I've just crossed the Mississippi River Bridge."

"Good. I bribed the bus driver to drop me off at LSU. I figured that would be one of the closest exits into the city coming in from Lafayette. We won't have time to eat but maybe we can grab a cup of coffee or find a quiet spot somewhere near the campus."

"I'd like that," Sabrina told him, her mind picturing a secluded area where they could sit and talk and just be together. Having spent four years at LSU as a student, John probably knew exactly where to find someplace like that.

"Take the Dalrymple exit, it'll bring you straight through. I'll be waiting for you at the visitors' center."

Gloriously, Dalrymple came before her patience wore out, easing her worry about making it to a bathroom. The narrow tree-lined street took her straight to LSU's visitors center and a sight of John she'd never forget. As Sabrina waited at the red light for the traffic to pass so that she could make a right turn, she had a moment to take him in. He stood outside the one story building at the corner of Dalrymple and Highland, looking so much like himself. His hands were in his jeans pocket but he was in no way relaxed. The tension in his broad shoulders held him stiff and straight. His fingers inside his pocket tapped out a nervous rhythm. Sabrina wondered what song was going through his head.

A horn blew, reminding her to pay attention to the traffic, causing John to turn toward her, his face instantly relaying exactly how happy he was to see her, making her forget about the traffic all over again, at least until the driver behind her reminded her yet again with a series of horn blasts.

Sabrina grinned, not letting the driver behind her get under her skin because John was already there. She eased into the turn and pulled into the visitors' center parking lot.

John was at her side, signaling her to roll down her window, barely giving her time to put the car in park and release her seatbelt.

"Come here," he said, leaning into the car window.

When Sabrina moved to open the door he shook his head. Reaching into the window he gently cupped a hand to each side of her face, his thumbs below each ear. He paused, then gave her the look.

The same one he used when blowing his trumpet.

But no, it wasn't the same.

This look was more intense.

And it was hers.

She really loved this man.

His lips were on hers a second later.

The moment he spotted her John knew it was all worth it.

The anticipation.

The wait.

The promise to be a one-man show for Brad, the bus driver, and his wife when they stopped in Shreveport. Sabrina was beautiful and she was his, not just because she wanted him but because he wanted her.

The ridiculous nervousness he felt at seeing her, since he now admitted to himself how he felt about her, evaporated as her lips moved across his. He needed her close.

His hands caressed her velvety skin as his tongue dove into her mouth, moving to her neck to lightly stroke on his journey to her shoulder. Wanting her closer, he pulled her toward him.

John had purposely kept her inside the car, wanting to erase the memory of James kissing her through the window from both their minds, replacing it with him. But now the car door was keeping him from feeling her. He wanted to feel 'Brina against him.

Without much thought beyond getting her into his arms without losing contact, his hand moved over her shoulders and under her arms, locking around her. Stepping back, he eased her out of the car through the window.

The movement was a precise and synchronized motion done without a word between them. It was as if he had played a tune that she danced to as the kiss deepened.

Horns blared as they locked their arms around each other, barely noticing anything else around them. Catcalls and a loud thump of something hitting the car drew them apart, only to come together again in an embrace that said more than words could have.

Unfortunately, necessity forced Sabrina to utter a few words.

"John, I've missed you like crazy and I'm exactly where I want to be but my bladder is insisting that I need to be in a bathroom."

Sabrina could feel the vibration before she heard and felt his laughter.

"Come on, there's a bathroom inside." He tucked her to his side and guided her toward the door. The building was dark and looked deserted. "It's pretty late. I don't think it's open."

"Oh, it had better be open."

"It's not open but someone's inside," he said, pressing his head against the pane in the door. "I know the guy, so I think I can convince him to let us use the facilities," he added with a playful look she'd seen on numerous occasions when he and his twin brother Josh were up to something.

A muffled, "There you go, John!" came through the door, which was opened by a young guy who had to be a college student.

"Hey, Drew."

As they shook hands and had a reunion, Sabrina slipped inside and found the restroom with no problem. By the time she finished her business, washed her hands and rejoined John, the room was empty.

"What happened to Drew?" Sabrina asked, curious but not caring too much. Now that her immediate need was taken care of she was aching to be back in his arms before they were interrupted again. Getting to that quiet place John had mentioned was top priority now.

"He's vacated the premises so that we can be alone."

"He has? That's wonderful."

"It was closing time and he's in charge of locking up. I arranged for him to finish the job once we're done with the place."

"I see," Sabrina said, scanning the spacious room, liking the idea that they didn't have to go searching for a place to be alone. But as she glanced around, she noticed the many windows. Earlier she hadn't cared where they'd go, only that she was in John's arms. Now, she'd like a bit of privacy.

" 'Brina, I know what you're thinking."

"And that is?"

"That you want to be alone with me without the whole world looking in."

"And how would you know that?"

"Because it's what I was thinking, and why I have a solution."

John took her hand and guided her around a wide circular desk in the middle of the room. Reaching the opening of the oval-shaped counter, Sabrina gasped. On the floor, laid out in the spacious area, were a blanket, a bottle of wine and a plate of cheese crackers.

"Please join me for a brief but romantic interlude."

"Most definitely," she answered, entering the area and taking a seat. The huge waist high counter surrounded them, providing the privacy she craved.

"The wine's not the finest but it was easy to find. The cheese crackers are a convenient and perfect blend of the traditional lovers' fare."

"Lovers' fare?"

"Cheese and crackers?" He picked up the paper plate to offer her a cracker.

Sabrina took one without thinking, one word sticking in her head. "Lovers?" she asked.

"Soon to be, I hope." He poured wine into clear plastic cups and handed her one. "You've been pretty quiet and most of what has come out of your mouth has been questions. Are you okay?"

"I'm overwhelmed, I suppose. It's only been a week since we've established ourselves as a couple."

"Established ourselves?" he chided.

"You know what I mean. We've just begun to get to know ourselves this way."

"I get what you're saying. Why do you think I ran?"

"I knew you wouldn't run for long."

"Because you know me so well."

"Of course."

"You aren't too overwhelmed, are you?"

"Just a bit, enough to say that I'm happily so. This *is* everything I've been dreaming of."

"A cheesy, thirty-minute picnic on the floor of LSU's visitors' center?"

"Exactly, especially since it's a cheesy, thirty-minute picnic with you."

John took the wine and the uneaten cracker from her hands and moved them to the side before opening his arms. Sabrina crawled between his outstretched legs and rested her back against his chest. "I feel exactly the same way," he told her.

They spent the next ten minutes taking in the feel of each other, the rhythm of their breathing in sync. Sabrina sat up, turned to face John, and spent a few minutes feeding him tiny orange cheese crackers and sips of wine. Her fingers lingered on his mouth, her lips tasting the wine from his own.

John reciprocated, the pad of his thumb tracing her bottom lip with gentle pressure, opening her mouth to taste the wine, then her lips, and finally the heated intensity between them. Minutes moved much too fast as he savored each kiss, each touch.

Lying on the blanket, they rested on their sides, facing each other, their eyes an intense reflection of what they felt for each other.

"I am so glad you came," John whispered in her ear.

"Since *you* finally began the chase."

" 'Brina, what am I going to do with you?"

"I'll have to think about that," she answered, already knowing the answer in her heart. She wanted to be a part of his life forever. Marriage was on her mind but she wasn't sure that it was on his.

A comfortable silence settled between them, only to be disrupted by the ringing of John's cell phone.

"That's my alarm." John stood and reached out a hand to help her get up. "James told me to be back at his mom's apartment by seven or he'd leave without me, taking my trumpet as a stand-in."

A halfhearted smile pushed the sides of her mouth up. "So, it's time?"

He nodded, pulling her close one last time. "I know, our time together was way too short. But I'll be back, and don't forget you can e-mail me and call me anytime you want."

Sabrina grinned up at him.

Without missing a beat he said, "I know this goodbye is a whole lot different than the last."

"A whole lot better."

"Come here."

"You've been saying that a lot."

"And you've been coming. I don't mess with what works."

"Then I advise you to add a *please,* or a *honey, baby,* or *sweetheart* to 'come here' if you want it to continue to work."

"Come here." He paused as if he was in deep thought. "Sugar foot."

No way was she going to be called sugar foot, and Sabrina let him know with a shake of her head and an "Are you serious?" stare.

"Baby cake? Honey bunch? My bebop?" He grinned after each suggestion.

"John, you've got to be kidding," she told him, handing him the cups to toss in the trashcan behind him. He began helping to clean up their mess, tossing paper plates and bending to fold the blanket they had used.

"How about Riff?" he asked, a serious expression on his face.

"Riff?"

"Short for riff tune."

"That clears things up," she said in exasperation, just now realizing how much she wanted a special name from him, a term of endearment. She hadn't realized that it would be this hard for him. 'Brina would have to do, she decided, turning to head toward the door.

"Wait." He laid a hand on her shoulders and pulled her back into him. "Let me explain."

Unable to help herself, Sabrina melted back into him. His soft breath whispered in her ear as he began his explanation.

"A riff tune is something special, 'Brina, unique to a jazz artist. It's a catchy tune, a signature phrase used to express the soul deep feeling when the music inside takes over." He began to sway from side to side, his hands at her hips, his voice a melody. "I never had a riff tune before, and now I understand why. I was waiting to catch you. It wouldn't come until I recognized that you were it. When I play," his hands went to her waist and turned her to face him, "my soul sings 'Sabrina.' You are my riff tune."

"Oh" was all she could say as his eyes relayed the sincerity of his words. Her body responded to them like a deep heated massage seeping into her, making her soft and pliable and so easy to bend and move in any direction he asked.

"Come here, Riff," he whispered, his mouth landing on her parted lips.

John's phone rang in the front pocket of his jeans. Refusing to release 'Brina he fumbled to answer it, knowing who it would be.

"Five minutes, Red," James's voice came through the phone.

"I'll be there." He clicked the phone closed and breathed "Riff" across her lips before taking them once more.

Driving John back to the bus to leave her was a bittersweet experience. Especially after the sensual explanation of his special word for her. She wouldn't trade it for the world. He could call her Riff any day.

John was exactly the way she wanted him. Exactly the way she had imagined that they could be, but circumstances were keeping them apart. They'd have time to be together later, she told herself as she pulled into the lot John directed her to and behind an air conditioned bus he'd soon board to leave her again.

Though it was hard, this parting was much more to her liking.

Sabrina followed him to the bus and stopped at the sight of James with his arms all over a tall, well-endowed woman with hips as broad as her breasts.

John moved past them and stepped onto the bus to talk to the driver. Sabrina followed but was stopped by James, who had spotted her.

"I hope you're not jealous." He winked at her.

"Not at all," she paused long enough to say, then turned to add, "Thanks, by the way."

"No, problem, mission accomplished." Then he went back to giving his undivided attention to the woman in his arms.

"Upset?" John nodded toward the couple.

"Not at all."

"Good. That's exactly what I wanted to hear," he said, introducing her to the driver, Brad, a big man with a shiny brown bald head and a heavy voice.

He showed her his "area" of the bus and much too soon she was standing outside giving him a final farewell.

As the bus departed from view Sabrina's phone rang. "I'll be catching you later, Riff," John said, his voice a full deep whisper sending the same thrill down her spine and melting of her muscles she had experienced a few minutes ago in his arms.

"You'd better," she said, heading to her car with no intention of allowing him to get off the phone for a very long time.

CHAPTER 11

They couldn't put it off any longer. The very next weekend Sabrina and Darren headed to New Orleans *without* Grammy. They had both agreed that it was best if they got a look at the house before allowing her to see the damage Katrina had done.

This was the house Grammy had chosen with her husband, in which she had raised her children and spent most of her adult life. She had been doing so well health-wise they didn't want to risk a setback caused by allowing her to see the destruction of her house. Sabrina was having trouble gearing herself up for what she expected to find. She had spoken to other evacuees at work and even perfect strangers standing in line at the bank, in Wal-Mart or the pharmacy about their experiences. None of them were pleasant; far from it. Sabrina was getting herself ready for what she knew would be an emotional day. She had tried to talk to John about it last night but instead had found them talking about the new song the band had practiced at rehearsal. She thought it was strange that he'd passed over her concern but simply put it down to John being excited about the new piece.

In order to get out of the house without Grammy figuring out where they were going and insisting on coming, Sabrina had arranged for her to go on an outing with Miss Faith and Diane. A Friday afternoon trip to a casino in Opelousas and an overnight stay with relatives of Miss Faith and Diane, would keep Grammy from knowing what they were up to. The older ladies saw it as a perfect opportunity to pump Diane full of questions and extol Darren's virtues. Sabrina almost felt sorry for Diane.

Darren had come home Friday night with a load of cleaning supplies, a rake, a shovel, masks and a variety of other tools in the back of his truck. She and he left the house early the next morning before the sun rose to avoid possible traffic. Sabrina had slept through the first hour of the trip, waking up when Darren pulled into a gas station.

"I need some coffee," Darren said. "Want some?"

A few minutes later, having settled into the cab of the truck again and armed with a warm shot of caffeine, Sabrina began to get her first bit of real information about him and Diane. She hadn't heard a thing about them since Grammy and Miss Faith's failed attempt to get the two together.

"I see you've been keeping contact with John," he commented. "The two of you straighten things out between you?"

"Pretty much," she said, folding her feet under her as she sipped her coffee, wondering if she dared to ask even as she found herself doing it. "How about you?"

"What about me?"

"You and Diane, have you worked out things between you?"

"There's nothing between me and Diane. And anyway, that's none of your business."

"You're right, it isn't," she said, knowing it was a long shot that he'd admit anything to her. She was his niece, and to him, still a kid.

After a long stretch of quiet and a half a dozen sips of coffee Darren said, "Why did you ask me about Diane? Has she said something to you?"

"She barely talks to me."

"Mmmm, Miss Prissy Pants. She thinks she's too much to talk to my niece!"

"She's not prissy, just well dressed, and she's not snooty or anything. I mean, she speaks when I speak to her but she's just not too friendly."

"She's stuck up and full of herself, thinking that dating a cop is too low grade."

"Did she say that?" Sabrina asked, noting the tightness around his mouth and the way his hands gripped the steering wheel. Sabrina didn't know Diane that well but she didn't have that impression of her. The woman just seemed unhappy and overwhelmed. That was it.

"Not exactly, but that's the way Miss Prissy Pants Diane thinks."

"Oh," Sabrina said, having no evidence to contradict what she felt might not be a good summation of Diane. It didn't matter what she said because he didn't seem to expect an answer. Instead, he dove right into asking questions about John, where he'd been and where he was headed, the kind of people he met.

This past week she had spent many late nights on the phone with John. They had talked about his gigs and her new job, his family and hers. He'd tell her about the people he'd met and the Katrina stories they'd shared with him and she'd tell him about her strange connection with people she didn't even know, their only common ground a hurricane named Katrina. She and John conversed with a natural ease. Sabrina paused in thought. Well, they talked with a natural ease most of the time. On some occasions John got really quiet at his end of the line, but not for long, which was why Sabrina never commented on it. But now she was remembering their odd conversation the night before. When she had brought up going to New Orleans and seeing the city in person for the first time, he had gotten really quiet before changing the subject. The more she thought about it, she realized that whenever she talked about going into the city there'd be a moment of uncomfortable silence before he changed the subject. Ah, maybe she was imagining things. John wasn't someone who was afraid of facing reality. He was even out there using his music to help people cope with their own present reality. She was probably imagining things. But she'd have to admit, it was usually after the weird silences that they'd end up talking about some strange things, sometimes completely trivial things. At least they were making contact.

Sabrina took a sip of coffee and shook her head, clearing it. She was making herself worry for nothing. They were at the beginning of a great relationship and getting to know each other on another level. That was all there was to that.

"I said, have John and his family gone into New Orleans to look at their property yet?" Darren almost yelled, as if he had asked the question a few times. He probably had.

"Scott, Devin and Mr. Calvin went a couple of weeks ago when they helped Randy and his family move to Gonzales. Ness said Scott and Devin will be in New Orleans this weekend with a crew to get some work started and they all are going to go in the following weekend. They asked if I'd mind babysitting then."

"All those kids?"

"I handle more at work every day."

"What about John?"

"He didn't say anything about going into the city." Once again she remembered that whenever she mentioned the condition of the city and going in to see her house he'd change the subject.

"I don't know. He didn't own any property, but he rented one side of a double. I'm sure he'll go in sometime to see what he can salvage. He's been way too busy to handle any of that," she said, wondering if she added it as an explanation to her uncle or an excuse.

"Mmm," was all Darren said to that. They rode in silence. A silence until they drove through Kenner, one of the surrounding communities of the greater New Orleans area. From Interstate 10 they could immediately see evidence of Katrina's mark: hotels without windows, buildings that were skeletons of steel and exposed studs, giving a view of nearly empty rooms with scattered remains of furniture. Blue roofs, temporary patches provided by the Corps of Engineers to prevent further damage by rainwater, were visible everywhere from their elevated viewpoint.

"Oh, my God."

"I can't believe it."

"Look at that!"

Yet the view from I-10 did not even begin to prepare her for what lay ahead.

Exiting the highway and entering familiar streets she had driven and walked on caused a tension of disbelief to twist in the pit of her stomach. All that she had seen on television, all that she had heard from others had not prepared her for the reality.

Her city was a desolate ghost town, a smelly, desolate ghost town. There was a stench in the air like none she had ever smelled. Rot, chemicals, a sourness hung in the air, penetrating the car despite the closed windows.

The refrigerators lining the curbs provided explanation for some of the stench that hung in the air. They were testament to the fact that people had begun the business of clearing out their homes to start over again. Because the flood waters had sat so long inside homes, they rotted from the inside. Gone were the memories of so many families. Her eyes began to overflow with silent tears. She let them fall.

Finally pulling up to the only home Sabrina had ever known, they both sat lost in their own thoughts. Her tears had stemmed themselves as she mustered the strength to face a more personal loss. She noted the watermark across the front of her home indicating the water had risen at least four feet high. There was a giant X spray-painted on the outside. Sabrina knew from others, and the news, that this meant the house had been checked for survivors, pets or dead bodies. That mark reminded her that her family had no bodies to bury because of this disaster, which helped her to put her feelings into perspective. They had been far luckier then other New Orleanians who had not only lost their homes, but their lives or those of their loved ones.

As the thought went through her head she felt her uncle take her hand.

"You ready to tackle some of this?" A deep sadness colored his words but determination showed on his face.

"About as ready as I'm ever going to be," she answered, attempting to mirror the strength she saw in his eyes.

After that there wasn't much conversation between them. They went to the back of the truck and began unloading. Darren handed her a mask, the big heavy plastic kind with a filter attached, and a pair of gloves. Then they walked inside.

"Careful," he told her just as her foot slid in the mud and gook that was a few inches thick on what was the living room floor. As they took an initial walk through the house it seemed as if the water had been determined to rearrange the furniture in every room. The sofa was in the kitchen, the rocking chair sat inside the bathtub, Grammy's favorite chair rested on top of the coffee table. Lamps and knick-knacks were scattered in places they had never been before. Sabrina wanted to take every item that was out of place and put it back where it belonged, recreate their home so that Grammy could return and see it the exact way that she had left it. But the thought was unrealistic and only lingered a second.

"Let's get started. We'll pick out what we can." Darren's voice was muffled but Sabrina nodded in understanding. They had their work cut out for them. What else could they do but begin?

Darren moved larger pieces of furniture out of the way as she picked through the mess to find the treasures of Grammy's that they could salvage. Sabrina began in Grammy's room with the top shelf of a closet. She was looking for the file of important papers, everything from birth certificates to shot records. The mold hadn't reached the large brown box. Sabrina took it out to the truck, returning with a few huge garbage bags to empty the closet, which was filled with mold. She tried not to look too long at the clothes she threw away. Some of them held precious memories: the hat Grammy always wore to church, the Christmas sweater she donned every Christmas Eve. Sabrina would have to remember to buy her a new one this year. The dress Grammy had worn to her eighth grade, high school and college graduations. She had said that it had cost so much that she was going to save it to wear to each one. And she had. Now it was garbage.

"You have the memories," Sabrina said out loud. "This is just stuff."

Sabrina told herself that over and over during the course of the morning as she went from room to room, the mask on her face slipping as she began to sweat. Despite it being officially fall, New Orleans remained warm and humid.

A few hours later, she had been able to salvage a box of memories, things that might seem silly to keep but those that Grammy would appreciate. She had also stacked Grammy's cast iron pots and pans which had been given to her by her own grandmother. They were a legacy Sabrina had no intention of leaving behind. Whatever she had to do to clean them and make them usable again she would do. She watched as her uncle stacked them in the back of his truck.

"Ready to take a break?" he asked.

Sabrina stood in the doorway staring at the small mountain of ruined furniture. The rocking chair Grammy had sat in while reading her stories and telling her tales of her mom, the sofa where Uncle Darren always sat to watch the games on Thanksgiving and tease her during commercials and half time. The chair Grammy always occupied as she sat waiting for Sabrina to return from some dance, date or outing with a friend. *They're all just things*, she told herself.

"Yeah," Sabrina finally said, pulling the mask from her face. "I feel a need to wash my whole entire body, but my hands will do. And I'm starving."

"Me, too. I didn't think about food. I hope we can find someplace to get something to eat."

"As deserted as it looks, I think we'll be lucky to find a place to buy a bag of chips."

The search for food took them on a journey past more destruction in Gentilly and Lakeview. They drove past City Park and its many destroyed trees.

"Uncle Darren, did you know that City Park has the largest natural stand of oak trees?"

"In the world or the U.S.?"

"I'm not sure," she said, wondering if it was the country or the world and if the fact was still true post-Katrina.

"We'll head toward the Central Business District. There wasn't much damage there so we should be able to find something to eat."

Sabrina nodded, weary of seeing the desolation around her. As they drove past the park and onto Esplanade Avenue, signs of life began to appear. First they noticed moving cars. None had passed their street the entire morning.

Then people.

Real people coming out of their homes.

These homes had no watermarks, but that didn't mean their home had no damage. Sabrina opened her window and waved, yelling, "Welcome back!"

"New Orleans!" a young couple yelled back to her. These people were some of the first to return to help rebuild their city. The tightness in her heart loosened a bit as she saw more and more evidence of people and life. It was going to take a long time to see that in most of the city, she knew, but it was reassuring to see it somewhere.

Sabrina had yelled to a least ten different people before Darren pulled to the side of the curb on Esplanade Avenue. "Why are we stopping here?"

"There's a Salvation Army truck and they're serving food. Come on."

That "come on" from Darren brought John to mind, lifting her spirits even more as she mentally added "Riff" to it. Sabrina didn't think she would ever be able to hear 'come on' without thinking of those moments with John.

Darren was already in line by the time she got out of the truck. The smell of barbecue had her stomach growling loudly.

"Sounds like you worked up an appetite," a voice said behind her. It was Scott, Ness's husband. Devin was right behind him.

"Shifting through a life's worth of memories will do that for you."

"We understand," Devin said as Darren handed her a closed Styrofoam plate.

"Devin, Scott, you want to join us for lunch?" Darren asked. "The Salvation Army's offering a nice meal here."

"We heard. Our workers have told us how well they've been feeding people," Devin said, raising the lid off on Sabrina's plate. "It looks as good as it smells."

"We'll be sitting in the back of my truck over there." Darren pointed across the street.

"How are things going at your place?" Darren directed the question to them after they settled in the bed of the truck.

Devin and Scott had lived next door to each other, having designed a French Quarter-style house with a connecting courtyard in the Lakeview area. Sabrina had babysat their kids a number of times over the last few years.

"Since we had eight feet of water in both our homes, it's almost like starting from scratch. But being owners of a construction company will make the job easier," Scott was saying.

"We've got our crew helping us move out most of the big things today in our house and our in-laws' houses. They'll be in next weekend to weed through the other stuff. Still up for a day of torture?" Devin asked, referring to the plan for her to babysit.

"You've got good kids," Sabrina defended, after swallowing a spoonful of beans and chicken. "They just like to have fun."

"That's the torture part," Scott said.

"They don't know when to stop having fun," Devin added.

Sabrina laughed, happy to have something to smile about.

They chatted as they ate. More about the kids, about John and relating a few tales about John and his twin Josh when they worked for the company during the summers when they were at LSU.

When the meal was over Scott asked, "How are things looking at your mother's house, Darren?"

"There's a lot to do."

"We know. Would you like a hand? We can send a couple of our crew to help you get the big stuff out," Devin added.

"You've got your guys working for you, not me."

"Consider it a favor," Devin began. "We've been trying to figure out the best way to help people. We've got ideas about rebuilding, and we're looking at some property in the Gentilly area to build reasonably priced homes, and rentals, for people who want to get back. But that's a long term proposition."

"We want to help people coming in now. We haven't worked out the details yet on how people would request the services and all, but we thought to send a few of our guys to various locations across the city to help move the big stuff out of people's homes so that their first time in wouldn't be so rough," Scott added.

"Like ruined furniture and refrigerators?" Darren asked.

"Exactly," they said together.

"You guys are wonderful!" Sabrina said, hugging them both.

"Make sure you tell Ness and Monica that," Devin said.

"Aw, they already know."

"Hey, there's nothing like being reminded once in awhile from an outside source," Scott insisted.

"I'm not an outside force. I'm like family."

They both nodded.

"We'll take you up on that offer," Darren told them.

Devin called two of his crew over, who hopped in the back of the truck.

With help from Prestway Construction Company, they finished their work for the day and were on the road again, headed back to Lafayette.

CHAPTER 12

There was no doubt in her mind.

John did not want to talk about New Orleans.

They would talk about the citizens of New Orleans and the hardships that they had gone through, the support he gave through his music, the help Devin and Scott were giving, how she, his sisters and mother gave aid at shelters, about Randy and his family. But he avoided all talk about the city itself.

The night she had returned from New Orleans her mind had been full of the images she had seen and the feelings they had provoked. So of course when John called, she had begun telling him about New Orleans, the city where they were born, the city they both loved. Half a dozen times there was that weird silence and a shift to talk about nothing in particular.

First it was a joke the bus driver had told him.

Next it was a comment about some little roadside restaurant they had stopped at for breakfast one morning.

Then James's girlfriend.

His trumpet.

The number of miles they'd traveled.

How many hotels they'd slept in.

"Stop, it, John. Just stop it," she finally told him.

"Stop what?"

"Stop changing the subject. I need to talk about today. I need to talk about what I've seen and heard. I need to talk about the mess our city's in."

"You do?"

"Yes, I do."

"Riff, I would rather talk about something else." He lowered his voice to the sweet, sexy whisper he'd used when he had first called her Riff.

"I would rather not," she said, knowing that he had used the name, and the tone, on purpose. He was trying to distract her again.

"Then I suggest we get off the phone." His voice was hard. He sounded like someone she had never met before.

"Why?"

"I don't see the point on harping on something we know is ruined. What's the use of moaning about the destruction of our city? Will doing that bring it back?"

"No, but it helps—"

"Helps who? You? I don't see how. It certainly doesn't help me."

"That's not what I was saying. Stop and listen to me."

"Not if all you're going to do is groan about the mess New Orleans is in. I don't want to hear about destroyed homes and torn up streets. When you want to talk about something else, call me."

"Maybe I won't call you at all."

And she didn't. For an entire week she didn't call, hurt by his attitude and the total disregard he'd shown for what she was feeling. This attitude was so uncharacteristic of the John she knew that Sabrina felt as if she needed to back away for a while. They were all under a lot of pressure from the various situations they found themselves in and on top of that, John was also dealing with adjusting to life on the road.

Towards the end of that week, a situation with one of her students helped her to put John's attitude into perspective.

Juwan was an eight-year-old boy with big, brown eyes and a personality you could see and feel as soon as he walked into a room. He was loveable, and helpful, and if she had been geared toward having a teacher's pet, he would have been hers. She was organizing a game of kickball for her third grade students that day and they were picking teams. There was a red team and there was a blue team.

Juwan immediately announced that he wanted to be on the blue team. As any good teacher would, she'd responded by saying, "You'll have to wait and see what team you'll be on."

Teams were being picked and, unlucky for Juwan, he was picked for the red team. Sabrina tossed him the ball, thinking to appease him by giving him the option of being the roller. When he caught the ball there was a look of rage that Sabrina would have never imagined on his face. "I want to be on the blue team!" he said, his voice elevating with each word. A roar came out of his mouth as he tossed the ball to the other side of the room. A second later he stood as still as a statue as tears ran down his face.

Sabrina directed the other students to have free play and went to him. She wrapped her arms around his shaking shoulders, knowing that there was more to this than not being picked for the team he wanted. He hadn't tried to hurt anyone; he'd thrown the ball into the corner of the gym where no one was.

"What's wrong, Juwan?" she asked.

"I wanted to be on the blue team."

"I know, but why?"

"Because I like the color blue."

"Any particular reason?"

"My room in New Orleans is—*was* blue and—" He paused for such a long time Sabrina didn't think he would tell her. "I wanna go home. I don't want to live in a shelter anymore. I want my house and my blue room. I picked out the paint and helped my mama paint the walls and we added sports stuff. And it was mine."

"I know." That was all Sabrina could think to say as she hugged the little boy who wasn't angry at her or his classmates; he was just angry at the way the world had changed. Who could blame him?

Hadn't she blown up? Didn't John deserve a chance to blow up?

On the ride home she considered calling John, but felt that she needed to give all her attention to the heavy traffic. Then she helped Grammy with dinner.

After dinner she sat with Grammy for a while, feeling as if she hadn't spent much time with her, and of course by the time they watched her favorite crime show it was much too late to call. John was probably already on stage.

Who was avoiding things now? she asked herself. She would call him tonight. By midnight he would have had time to settle down after the show.

"So Grammy, what have you been up to?" Sabrina asked to pass the time.

"I should ask what you've been up to. But no, I don't need to ask. I know," she told her, not taking her eyes off the television.

"And what do you know?"

"That you and Darren went to New Orleans to see the house. It's my turn. We can go when you're off for Thanksgiving break."

"Sure, Grammy," Sabrina answered, knowing not to argue when Grammy took that tone. By then the house would have been gutted, cleaned out completely, thanks to Scott, Devin and the Prestway Construction Company. "Do we need to go before Thanksgiving or after?"

"After, I don't want to ruin my holiday. Are we still going to spend Thanksgiving with Joyce and Calvin and their wild gang?"

"Yes," Sabrina laughed.

"Good, I'm ready for some excitement and fun. It's boring, way too boring, around here. And dealing with two hardheaded adult children who couldn't see love if it bit 'em is frustrating."

"Sorry, Grammy."

"Don't you worry, I'll think of something. Faith's coming over because Diane has some fancy thing to go to for work. We plan on hashing it out over a game of cards."

"I wish you luck."

"At least you and John have worked things out." Grammy wore a pensive expression. "Wait a second, I haven't heard you whispering and shrieking on the phone for quite some time. What's going on?"

"Not a thing. There's the door. It must be Miss Faith." Sabrina dashed to the door and let Miss Faith in. Miss Faith headed straight to the den, saying nothing. "Hi, Diane, you look beautiful." And she did, in a slinky black dress that shouted classy.

"Thanks." She gave Sabrina a half grin. "I'll be back for you in a couple of hours, Mama."

"Take your time," Miss Faith called back.

"Have a good time," Sabrina said.

Diane paused, turned to her and asked, "You don't like me much, do you?"

"I don't know you," Sabrina answered, completely surprised by the question.

"But what you *do* see, you don't like?"

"Not at all, you just seem intense."

"Oh. Okay. Thanks." And then she was gone.

Weird, Sabrina thought, going to the kitchen to brew some coffee and fix a tray with slices of cake for Grammy and Miss Faith. The trick would be to leave the tray and not hang around long enough to be questioned. Which she did with minimal attention to herself. "Goodnight, ladies," she said with a sigh of relief.

Grammy's voice followed her down the hall. "We'll be working on you later."

Sabrina went to the enclosed sun porch. She had cleared it out and taken it over as her room. Playing a soft jazzy tune she did a few warm-ups and went into a freestyle kind of dance, allowing her body to go where the music took her. An hour later, feeling invigorated, she took a shower and hopped into her jammies. She peeked in at Grammy and Miss Faith, who were engrossed in their card game, and went back into the room to wait until it was late enough to call John.

Just as she was about to settle into her bed to listen to the jazz CD John had given her, the phone rang. Taking a peek at the clock she noticed that it was only ten o' clock. John wouldn't be calling this early if he was calling.

When it stopped after two rings Sabrina figured Grammy had answered and crawled to the middle of her bed to relax.

"Sabrina!" she heard just as she was getting comfortable.

Hearing the doorbell ring Sabrina went to the door instead of grabbing the phone that Grammy held out to her. "Tell whoever it is to hold on," Sabrina said to her grandmother, opening the door for Diane who followed her into the den. "Who is it?" Sabrina asked as she reached for the phone.

"One of Darren's patrolmen. Darren's at the hospital and—" Grammy began only to be interrupted by a high-pitched screech.

"The hospital!" Diane yelled as the screech died down. Before anyone could react she began asking questions. "What happened? What's going on? I told that crazy man he'd get killed. I told him I couldn't stand by and watch him put his life on the line every day of his life, the stupid fool. Stay here, Mama, I'm going." And she was gone as quickly as she had come.

"Is Uncle Darren hurt?" Sabrina asked.

"I never said that." Grammy had the phone nestled in her lap in such a way that Diane's outburst had to have been muffled. "But this could work." Putting the phone to her ear she said to the patrolman, "Tell Darren that someone's coming for him."

As she hung up the phone she and Miss Faith cackled with glee.

"I told you we only had to wait for an opportunity," Miss Faith said as Sabrina left the room shaking her head.

As long as Darren wasn't hurt, she saw no reason to warn him. Crawling back into the middle of the daybed, Sabrina listened to the jazzy beat that reminded her so much of John she almost felt as if he were there helping her to forgive him because she truly knew him better than he knew himself. She'd call him in a little while, she thought as she drifted off to sleep.

"Red, what's going on with you?" James asked as John made it to his room. "Ya' losing it. Get it back!" was all he said before going into his own.

Oh yeah, John knew he was losing it. He was losing it because he had let Sabrina under his skin and she had dug her way in deep and wanted him to pull at things he wasn't ready to pull at, let alone examine.

He shouldn't have gotten so angry.

He should have listened.

He always listened.

John had always been the considerate, the patient twin. The one who always cared what other people thought. But now that he'd gotten involved with a beautiful woman he'd become his twin brother Josh.

Josh, who he hadn't talked to since right after Katrina.

Josh, who he was avoiding because he knew Josh would have told him off. Told him to get off his butt and face the fact that New Orleans was in ruins and do something about it. After all, they both had the skills, having learned the construction business from their brothers-in-law.

But he wasn't himself. He hadn't been since the hurricane, and for some reason talking about the city and even thinking about going there to face it all was something he didn't want to do. Something he felt he couldn't do. Not yet. Thanks to the Jazz Foundation he had a job. He was working and helping evacuees cope through his music, bringing a bit of New Orleans culture to homesick citizens all across the country. He would continue to help this way. He'd face the city when he was ready, even though his behavior made him feel immature and needy.

There was one way he could feel less like a fool. He would call Sabrina. He should have called her back right after he made that stupid statement. But he didn't and now he was missing her so much, it was affecting his music. He wanted her back. Even if all they had was a phone connection he wanted it. He needed his Riff.

Laying his trumpet on the floor, he dug in his pocket for his cell phone and dialed her number.

"Do you know what it means?" Sabrina was on stage, singing in a dark smoky lounge. John was playing his trumpet. She draped her body over his as she sang, sexual tension passing between them as her fingers grazed his chest, his shoulder, walked through his close cut hair.

"Sabrina! Answer your phone!" Grammy called from her room.

Sabrina woke up and automatically did as she was ordered. "Hello?" she said, a sleepy haze hanging over her.

"Hello yourself, Riff."

"John?" She had been dreaming about him. He was playing and she was dancing all over him. The moves they were making together were like foreplay. And she had been thinking a lot about foreplay and making love even though they hadn't spoken for an entire week. And his voice, it sounded so sexy, exactly in tune with the way he had played his trumpet in her dream.

"Did I wake you?"

"Yes."

"Do you want to talk?"

"Yes."

"I'm liking your answers. This could be a good time to ask you anything."

"Yes," she said, and they both laughed.

"I've missed you, Riff."

"I've missed you, too," she admitted, the conversation moving in the direction she had hoped.

"I didn't mean to blow up at you last week."

"I understand. You had a right to. Remember when I blew up with you?"

"You didn't blow up at me, you just blew."

"True."

"I didn't have the right to shut you down."

"Actually, John, that was the only part that hurt my feelings. You have always been there for me and now that we're a couple I'm expecting us to be there for each other even more."

"Exactly."

"But then I realized something else."

"What was that?"

"I was so worried about how I wanted you to be there for me that I wasn't thinking about being there for you."

"How?"

"By honoring your need to *not* talk about New Orleans."

"Still, I should have listened. I'm just not ready to dive right into the whole destruction of New Orleans."

"You will be, and when you're ready I'll be there."

"Whew, I'm glad we had this conversation," he said.

"We should have had it days ago."

"I agree. What do you want to talk about now?

"One of Brad's jokes?"

"They're always corny."

"How about telling me about the dive you ate in for dinner."

"They're all the same."

"James's girlfriend."

"Which one?" he asked. "Actually I would say none of the above, Riff. Let's talk about us."

"Us, it is," Sabrina said, settling down in the middle of her bed, satisfied with their reconciliation and anticipating the next time she would see him. Christmas really wasn't that far away.

CHAPTER 13

Thanksgiving held a whole new meaning for all victims of Hurricane Katrina. Everyone had losses, some more severe than others, but there were also thanksgivings: survival stories, unselfish acts of compassion from neighbors and perfect strangers alike, a new appreciation and love for life and home, even a home that couldn't be lived in.

Sabrina thought to embody the spirit of thanksgiving with a dance performance. She had been practicing a variety of dances with every grade level, a challenging task but right up her alley. Concentrating her mind on choreographing and evening practices that went beyond her after school program kept her from missing John as much.

Sabrina had enlisted the aid of the middle school math teacher, a fellow New Orleanian who had fifteen years of experience in dance. Gerard Baptiste was amazing. He helped with her after school students and seemed to know exactly what she was thinking and how to inspire the kids to give it one more shot. At the end of the day, having worked with five to six groups of kids in her PE classes, Sabrina was exhausted, and his help was invaluable.

It was the Thursday before Thanksgiving break and the performance was scheduled for the next day. Being ambitious, Sabrina had added a lift to one of the dances to symbolize New Orleans rising from the floodwaters of Katrina. It was a simple lift but a combination of adolescent sixth grade embarrassment and nerves interfered with progress. Every other part of the dance was beautifully synchronized, all except the lift. Sabrina was at a point where she was ready to give it up and scratch it from the routine when Gerard stepped in.

"Joe, you can do this," he said to the young boy who would be lifting a petite classmate Sabrina had chosen as the liftee. "Don't be afraid of the girl. She won't bite you. Will you bite him, Ashley?"

Ashley shook her head, having no problem with being lifted.

"Would it help if you had an example to go by?"

Joe nodded.

"Okay, Miss Adams, let's show these young people the technique."

"You got it, Mr. Baptiste."

Sabrina twirled to the other side of the room, demonstrated the series of dance steps that preceeded the lift. Gerard's hands held her securely at her waist, as she glided into his arms before landing safely again. The kids gave a standing ovation. Sabrina knew her face was split wide open with a grin of appreciation. "Thanks, Gerard," she leaned close to whisper before organizing her students to perform the last sequence of steps that would lead into the lift.

Standing to the side, she nervously watched as Joe got into position, lifted and gently released his partner, maybe not as flawlessly as she had hoped but with more confidence and success than he had before.

"Can we do it one more time?" Joe asked.

Sabrina nodded. As the other students packed their belongings she watched as they practiced the lift not once more but at least a half dozen times, only stopping because Ashley was getting tired of being lifted.

"I'll take these guys to the cafeteria for checkout," Gerard told her, taking the entire group of kids with him, Joe and Ashley bringing up the rear.

Excited by this little achievement, Sabrina sashayed across the floor, throwing in a twirl or two, stopping short when she spotted a body that she was about to run directly into.

"John!" she said, barely catching herself in time. "What are you doing here?" she asked, wrapping her arms around him and holding him close. He felt so good. He was real and in her arms.

"Come here, Riff," he said, leaning back an inch or so to lift her chin with his thumb, raising her lips to his.

She was so lost in John's kiss and his scent that she didn't realized that someone had entered the gym until he pulled back and whispered, "Your friend's back."

"Oh, Gerard, sorry about that. Thank you."

"I was just coming to walk you to your car."

"No. I mean, I'm okay, thanks," she told him, noticing a look of disappointment on his face. Despite knowing she hadn't done anything to indicate that there was more to their relationship than friendship, Sabrina began to feel guilty.

"I'll take care of her."

"Yes, John will take care of me. Oh, yeah, meet John, my boyfriend," Sabrina said, realizing that this was the first time she had introduced John to anyone as her boyfriend. Noting the downward turn of Gerard's mouth, Sabrina decided that somebody should leave. Now.

"You teach here?" John asked, pulling her even closer to his side than she already was, which was ridiculous because she couldn't get any closer to him.

"Yes, with Sabrina. I'm a math teacher."

"And dancer."

"You saw the lift?" he asked.

"I saw the lift. I hope you won't be needing to do any more demonstrations," John said. His eyebrows furrowed and his face held a stern expression she'd never seen before.

"John," she whispered, tapping him on the shoulder.

"Only at the lady's request."

"I don't recall her requesting this time."

"John!" she said again. "How long were you here?"

"Long enough."

"Well, then, Sabrina, I'll see you tomorrow," Gerard said, backing out of the gym.

"John, that was rude."

"I know. I came here to surprise you because I missed you so much I was aching inside and when I walk in, what do I see, but some guy with his hands on you. I couldn't help myself, Riff."

"You'd better learn how," Sabrina said, twisting to face him.

"Forgive me?"

"Only if you promise never to act like that again."

"Can't promise. All I can do is try."

Sabrina stared long and hard at him. "Are you sure you're not Josh? You're starting to sound more and more like your twin brother."

"Naw, you'd know if I were Josh. It's just a dormant side of me that rises when some strange man has his hands on my woman."

"Your woman?"

"*My woman,*" he repeated.

Sabrina laughed, wrapping her arms around his neck, not really minding being called his woman. "Well then, *my man,* I'll accept that. For now." She laid another lengthy kiss on his lips, pulling back as she remembered that they were in the middle of an elementary school gym. "So tell me. How were you able to make it back and how long will you be here?"

"Wondering how long you have to put up with me?"

"No, wanting to know how long I'll have the pleasure of your company."

"Ten days. A gig was cancelled and James took that as a sign that we should spend Thanksgiving with our families. Then after Thanksgiving we play at some club in Baton Rouge. Care to join me there?"

"I'd love that."

"Well, then, come on, Riff. Let's get out of here. I'll take you to dinner."

Sabrina turned to grab her backpack that John promptly slung onto his shoulder, tucking her close to his side as they left.

"How did you get here?"

"Brad dropped me off at your uncle's house, who I saw with his hands all over some woman. Talk about needing to toss water on someone . . ."

Laughing, Sabrina said, "That had to be Diane."

"The Diane who was at dinner with us after the Yambilee concert? The one who acted like she hated your uncle?"

"Exactly. Turns out she was in love with him."

"Could have fooled me. Of course I was pretty busy trying to survive the attack of the grannies."

"That's true. But it's definitely love. Diane thought Uncle Darren was shot and dying in the hospital, so she rushed over to be with him. The rest is history."

"That's something." He shook his head. "Anyway, your uncle told me you were still at work and he offered to drop me here."

"Nice."

"I'd say so. I'm beginning to believe he won't do me bodily harm for laying hands on his niece."

"Right now, he can't talk," Sabrina said, unlocking the door. "I can't go into a room without finding him and Diane all over each other. It can't be easy for them with Miss Faith in her house and me and Grammy in his. But man alive, it's ridiculous."

They soon came to know the exact frustration her uncle and Diane experienced. There was no real place for them to be alone. After dinner they went to her uncle's house. Grammy and Miss Faith were watching their crime show in the den. Darren and Diane were in the living room. Both Diane and Miss Faith were spending the night because their house was being fumigated. Grammy had a no boys/boyfriends-in-the-bedroom rule which extended to Darren despite the fact that she was living in his house, so Sabrina and John sat on the porch, huddled in the swing, stealing kisses and enjoying the novelty of talking and touching at the same time. No one seemed to want to go to bed that night so the house never got quiet. They had to be content with a few heated kisses before Brad swung by to pick John up about midnight.

After his rehearsal, John came to the school and caught the last part of the performance, successful lift and all. Gerard made a point of avoiding John, making Sabrina feel guilty all over again, but not enough to give it more than a moment's notice. She was full of the excitement of having John with her for the holidays. Talk about something to be thankful for.

Since she was off for the entire week, they had decided that she would go with him to Gonzales to stay with his family until Thanksgiving Day, when Darren and Grammy would come over for the day. Miss Faith and Diane would be spending the day with relatives in Opelousas, which didn't make Darren too happy. They may as well have announced that they were going to get married and spend the rest the of their lives together since it looked like that was where they were headed. That was exactly where she wanted to head, but she and John had yet to discuss anything so far into the future.

The mob welcome should have been an indication of what their time would be like with the Lewis clan. With the additional family members that converged for the holidays, it seemed as if an entire community had descended on Sabrina and John when the front door of the middle house of the three occupied by relatives opened.

They were hugged and squeezed and kissed. Some of the family John hadn't seen since before Katrina, some Sabrina hadn't seen for over a year, evidenced by the fact that little Jax, Daniel and Cassie's daughter, was now running around with the big little kids. She'd been a babe in arms the last time Sabrina had seen her. Teresa was no longer pregnant but had her arms around a wiggling bundle who was reaching for Trey, the daddy. Both little girls were the product of mixed parentage, apparent by the combination of features and skin color, but it made no difference. They were nothing more then relatives and cousins to have fun with in this extended family.

"Boy or girl?" Sabrina asked Teresa of the chubby baby with stray wisps of black hair when the excitement of welcoming another family member had died down.

"Girl, we're trying to even the numbers here," she said, pointing her head in the direction of all the boys. "Poor Blaze is outnumbered. She needed a few girl cousins to even things out."

John wrapped his arms around Sabrina and they followed everyone into the center house that remained

John's parents temporary home as well as that of Randy and his family. Other family members were living in the two houses flanking the one where they gathered.

"Wait a minute, Uncle John! Sabrina!" Vicki shouted behind them.

Everyone turned to see what the problem was. Some of the family who had gone inside came out again to see what was going on.

"Are you girlfriend and boyfriend, now?" Vicki asked, her hands on her little hips, her blonde ponytail swaying with each word.

"Oh-oh," Ness whispered. "Vicki's been proposing to John since she was four years old," she explained to Sabrina.

"I understand the compulsion," Sabrina said.

Vicki walked up to John and took his empty hand in one of her own, her eyes serious and intent. Everyone waited to see how the scene would play out, having witnessed Vicki's proposals over and over again.

He stooped down and, looking directly into her eyes, simply said, "Yes."

After a long pause during which her eyes darted from John to Sabrina, she sighed and said, "If you had to have a girlfriend I'm glad that it's Sabrina."

Everyone laughed as they headed back into the house.

Later that day Vicki came up to Sabrina and asked, "Are you going to ask John to marry you?"

"I think I'll let him do the asking."

"Do you want him to?"

Sabrina nodded.

"I'll teach him how. He's never asked me, even after all the times I've asked him," she sighed in exasperation.

Sabrina smiled as she watched the little girl rejoin her cousins and brothers as they rolled around the floor with their dads.

"What was that all about with Vicki?" John asked a few minutes later.

"Girl talk."

Sabrina had a few other opportunities for girl talk with the Lewis women when they all disappeared to have coffee at Ness's house after dinner.

"Aren't they going to miss us?" Sabrina asked.

"They're getting what they deserve," Monica said. "I warned Devin about letting the big little kids have too much sugar. The consequence of allowing small children to have a double dose of cookies *and* ice cream is overactive, overexcited kiddies who will *not* want to sleep tonight."

"Which means?"

"A dad who is going to have a tough time getting them to bed."

"You won't help?" Teresa asked.

"I won't lift a finger," Monica declared.

"Neither will I," Ness said. "I saw Scott giving ours second helpings of both."

"Poor guys," Cassie said. "I don't have to worry about Daniel giving Jax too much sugar. He monitors it himself."

"Good for Daniel. And don't feel sorry for Scott and Devin. They've done this before and still haven't learned their lesson."

"That's because we gave in and took over," Ness admitted.

"Not tonight. Listen, here they come," Monica said.

Sabrina sat back to watch a couple of pros in action.

"There's Mommie!" Devin said with an enormous look of relief on his face. Scott followed behind, pointing and yelling, "Mommie's here!

"Mommie! Mommie! Mommie!" The toddlers bounced all around their mothers, who gave them hugs and kisses.

"Bath time, and then bed," Monica announced.

"I was hoping you'd say that," Devin said, plopping onto the overstuffed sofa.

"Oh no, Devin, please don't relax. Take our sugar-fortified children and get them ready for bed. I'll take care of our other children."

"Whoa! Dev, she said please in that oh-so-polite voice we love."

"I know," he told Scott.

"I think you're in trouble."

"It was just a little ice cream and a few cookies," Devin said, as the boys hopped onto his back, literally climbing him, while Blaze latched onto his leg, jumping up and down, begging him to walk.

"I see. Thank you. Which means that you won't have any problems taking care of the results of a little ice cream and a few cookies," Monica said before leaving the room.

"Brown Eyes," Devin called to his wife.

"She said thank you, Bug," Scott said, using Devin's nickname to tease. "You *are* in trouble," he repeated as his own sons raced around him.

"What about you?" Devin asked, looking pointedly at Ness, who didn't look too happy herself.

"MyNessa," Scott began, then hesitated before continuing, "why don't we go home and put our kids to bed so that we can . . ." He came over, nearly tripping over Kacey or maybe Kyle, and whispered something in her ear.

"The girls and I will be home in about an hour or so," Ness told him. "Maybe by then the extra sugar will have run its course. If you're still alive we can talk about your suggestion."

"Looks like you are in a heap of trouble yourself, my man," Devin told his friend as they went their separate ways.

The ladies enjoyed a good laugh. John walked in a minute later. "There you are," he said. "What was Scott mumbling about?"

"You'll have to ask him," Sabrina said.

"Do you want to go for a walk?" His eyes were full, giving her an idea of what going for a walk really meant. She didn't hesitate to agree.

"I'd like that," she said, taking his outstretched hand. "See you later, ladies," she called as she went away with John, unable to keep herself from smiling and thinking about the possibility of John with their kids and his family at a gathering similar to this one.

"Are you having a good time?"

Nodding, she answered, "I love your family. I always have a good time with them."

"I'm happy to hear that," he said, the slight frown marring his face at odds with the comment.

"Are you sure you're happy to hear that?" she asked, as they walked down the graveled driveway.

"Of course," he answered, drowning out that annoying little voice that had him wondering if the attraction she felt was more for his family than for him. She'd spent more time with them since they became a couple. Not that it could be helped.

"John?"

"What?"

"I ask, not that it really matters, but where are we going?"

"Away." He took in the lopsided grin on her face and smiled right back at her as he tossed aside the foolish thoughts he was having about Sabrina and his family.

"Away?"

"Away. From the family and noise and watchful eyes."

"Oh. To do what?"

Beyond the light coming from the porch he turned her so that her back was against someone's SUV, one of the many vehicles in the driveway. "This," he said, before pressing his body into hers. Sabrina felt the hardness of his thighs against her and a few seconds later, the throbbing hardness between his legs as he kissed her with a depth of emotion that told her how much he wanted her, as if she couldn't tell from the wealth of other evidence.

A flood of headlights and the crunching sound of a car pulling into the driveway next door pulled them apart.

"I wonder who that is?" Sabrina asked, not really caring, her forehead resting on John's as she worked on evening out her breathing.

"Eyes. More watchful eyes," he growled. "Will I ever get you to myself?"

"John? Is that you?"

"Josh," he said, turning to his twin brother who was two steps behind. Their hands slapped together in a high five that merged into a hug and a pounding of each other's back as they both talked at the same time. Sabrina stayed where she was, her back against the SUV as she noted their marked similarities and outstanding differences. Josh was about a half inch taller than John and had a slightly thicker build. His face more easily rolled into a grin and he was notorious for his practical jokes. John, though not as muscular as Josh, was not slight. A heated pulse went through her thinking about his solid thighs pressed against her. He was strong, just not blatantly so. And his strength didn't stop there. It showed in his serene gentleness, except when he was warning away other men, and his stoic nature.

"And so who do we have here?" Josh was saying. "My brother's got a girl? My twin brother's got a girlfriend? Why didn't I sense this momentous event? What happened to 'My music is my woman'?"

"My woman happened to it. You know Sabrina."

"The Pest."

"No more, Josh," Sabrina told him.

At the same time John said, "Don't call her that."

"Well, look at you," Josh said, obviously deciding not to respond to what either of them had said. "You're all grown up."

"It happens," she said, leaning toward him to give him a quick peck on the cheek. She liked Josh. He was a clown with a good heart, but a clown nonetheless.

"Congratulations, you two. Finally found a way to really feel like part of the family, huh? Remember when you begged Ness to adopt you?"

"Do you forget anything?" Sabrina asked, wanting to shake him. Leave it to Josh to remember something like that.

"Anybody still up? I haven't seen anyone since Pre-Katrina."

"Oh, most everybody is still awake, which explains why we're out here," John said, tucking her to his side as they headed back to the center house. "How are things in Atlanta?"

"Pretty good. I've adjusted, but I think I'll be able to move back to New Orleans soon. Bell South's re-opening its offices and wants me to return at the beginning of the next year."

"Why would you want to do that?"

"Because New Orleans is my home. We grew up there, remember? You know how it feels, it's a seeps-into-your-soul kinda place. Listen to me. I don't have to explain it to you. You're the one who normally waxes poetic about New Orleans and jazz. You already *know* what I mean without me having to explain it. You're the artist, my big time jazz-playing twin. Hey everybody!" he called out as they got to the front door. "Josh has finally made it!"

"Uncle Josh!"

"Josh!"

"Look who's here!
"Hey, little brother!"
"That boy's finally remembered he's got a family!"

As the night wore on, John found himself extremely content. His mom made pina coladas and his dad passed out cold beer as they all chatted and kidded with each other, catching up on what was happening in each other's life, Post-Katrina of course. Soon Sabrina's head rested on his shoulder and not long after he felt the soft, even rhythm of her breath warming his chest.

"Why don't I show Sabrina to her room?" his mom was saying.

He wanted to tell her no, that she was okay right where she was. John loved the feel of her sleep-warm body resting against him. But everyone else was moving and heading off to bed.

"Where is she sleeping?' he asked.

"Don't tell him, Mama. We can't have him sneaking off to visit his girlfriend in the middle of the night."

"You stop trying to cause trouble, Joshua Michael. John wouldn't do anything to disrespect the values we have in our family. Right, John?"

"Of course not, Mama," he said, scratching the idea of sneaking into her room when everyone was sleeping just to hold her in his arms a little longer, not that he didn't have other things in mind. Despite what Josh had said earlier, he had had other girlfriends, just not girls that he had become serious with. They were more like groupies who wanted to be with him because of his musical talent. Sabina was a girlfriend like no other. He thought about her constantly, he wanted her constantly, which was why he had been so jealous of that Gérard guy. He wanted to tear her clothes off and feel her naked body against his own. He also wanted to savor her with sweet, slow strokes and gentle touches, and he didn't want to pressure her. It was a good thing there was so much family around. It left John little room to do anything at all.

"John, don't just stare her awake, give her a little shake," his mom suggested.

"Sabrina, wake up," John said, stroking her shoulder.

Her eyes shot open. "What?"

"You need to get to bed."

"With you?" she whispered.

From the smirk on Josh's face it was loud enough for him to hear it, too.

"No, my mom will show you your room. I think it's different from where you slept before."

"Okay," she said, leaning into him to give him a tender kiss before standing. John held her hand and stood with her. "See you in the morning," she said, appearing to be more awake as she followed his mother.

"If the two of you get married, she'll fit right in. The Pest—"

"Look, Josh, get used to saying Sabrina."

"Sabrina's almost a part of the family already. Joining up legally will make her good and happy," Josh continued.

"You said something like that already. What are you talking about?"

"Well, think about. She's never had much of a family. She's always been around ours. She called Ness her sister for about a year or so. Sabrina's just a nice, easy fit. That's all I'm saying."

"You're drunk."

"Nope, I've just got a little buzz. Look, you don't want to think about it, don't think about. I'm rambling anyway because I'm drunk."

"Go to bed, Josh. You know we're going to have to defend our basketball title with those two old men tomorrow."

"Scott and Devin? They don't stand a chance. Besides, I didn't see a basketball goal."

"They're setting up a portable one tomorrow and getting their crew to build a court in the backyard this coming week."

"I better get some sleep then. Good night," Josh said, making his way to the guest room that they would be sharing.

Not feeling the least bit tired and knowing that he wouldn't be able to sleep with a live and in person Sabrina in the same house, John lingered in the den, flipping through the channels, trying to keep himself from thinking about what Josh had said about Sabrina always wanting to be a part of their family.

It was insignificant to how they felt about each other. So what if she enjoyed being with his family? He enjoyed being with his family. It was just that Josh's words reflected the exact same thoughts he'd been having himself.

CHAPTER 14

The days flowed into each other with a natural rhythm and pace that Sabrina found to be energetic and comforting. She spent the early part of the day with John during his rehearsal sessions in Baton Rouge. They would wake up at about the same time Randy left the house to head to New Orleans. She and John would take the thirty minute ride in the opposite direction to meet the band in Baton Rouge. They would spend three to four hours at rehearsal, grab something for lunch and take it to a quiet, secluded place on LSU's campus or elsewhere to indulge in being with each other, ending up being more hot and bothered than appeased and satisfied by the time they headed back to Gonzales where the fun always began again. Sabrina was so comfortable with every member of the family. She knew she was jumping the gun, but secretly considered them her family already.

Often she caught John giving her a strange look at odd times, when she was coloring with the kids or helping Vicki, Megan, Jazz and Tiara fine tune a cheer they had made up for Thanksgiving, or the time when she and John's sisters, cousins and sister-in law broke out in song after having an argument about the name of the family band who sang the "O-O-H Child" song.

"I'm not concerned about who wrote it. I want to know the words," Monica said.

"It's easy," Ness said and began to sing.

Sonya had left the room and come back with a CD player blasting the song. "Randy saved it from the floodwater and it still plays, listen. It's by the Five Stair Steps."

They all got up to dance and sing, the kids becoming their audience. Josh and John walked in just as they finished the song.

"That should be our theme song," Josh told them. "Things have *got* to get easier."

John didn't say a word to her and Sabrina dismissed his look because when they were alone together she had his undivided attention, and the looks he gave her then were anything but weird.

After rehearsal on Wednesday they planned to not return to Gonzales until late that night, after the gig. James broke the practice session early and they loaded up the bus.

"Why are we leaving so early?" Sabrina heard John ask Brad.

"Ask James," was all Brad had said.

When John did find James, he asked him the same question, but all he said was, "You'll see, Red," making this gig seem mysterious and giving him an uncomfortable foreboding that he wasn't going to like where they were going.

They settled in the bus, Sabrina taking a seat next to John. It wasn't long until he did see. "We're going to New Orleans to play," John said, realizing that it was exactly what he had suspected. His hard, angry eyes bore into James's back.

"You got it, Red," he said without turning around.

"I don't want to play there."

"I know it, but we all have to do a lot of things we don't want to do. Sometimes it's the bitter medicine that cures what ails us."

"Humph," was all John could bring himself to say for a long time. He thought about his options. He was starting to feel desperate, so desperate they he considered getting off the bus and walking back to Baton Rouge where they had left Sabrina's car. But it would be dangerous and much too far to walk on the highway and he wasn't going to do that to Sabrina. He could simply refuse to play, but what would that say about him? Not wanting to admit it, he realized that James was right: Sometimes you had to do things you didn't want to do.

Sabrina took the hand that was lying limply on his lap. John knew he was being pathetic and cowardly with this resistance about going into New Orleans. He knew that he would eventually have to face up to it.

He simply didn't want to.

He hadn't geared himself up for it. He hadn't prepared his mind for the almost complete destruction of places he'd been and seen, areas that had deep meaning to him. He felt sweat beading on his forehead and sliding down his neck and back. A moistness lay between their entwined hands, but Sabina didn't release his. He couldn't look at her because he hated this weakness inside himself. That was one of the main reasons he had gotten so angry with her all those weeks ago.

"Where are we playing?" he asked no one in particular.

"Fat Harry's," one of the other guys answered.

"That's on Saint Charles near the Central Business District. There wasn't much damage there."

"I know, that's why we're taking a ride through the Ninth Ward before setting up at Fat Harry's," James answered, giving him a hard look before glancing out the window again. "There's been talk about Harry Connick, Jr. and Branford Marsalis working toward organizing the building of a Musicians' Village so everyone can come home. Don't you wanna come home, Red?"

Harry Connick, Jr. and Branford Marsalis, both natives of New Orleans and jazz legends in their own right, were doing more than helping people cope. They were working to give other musicians a leg up, same as the Jazz Foundation which kept them working. "Of course," John finally answered. Eventually, maybe a few years from now, he thought to himself. He felt too vulnerable at the moment to follow Harry and Branford's lead. Maybe he would, when he didn't have to see the waste and destruction of the places he loved.

The rest of the drive on Interstate 10 was solemn, like a funeral. The bus was filled with a sort of painful silence no one felt the need to break because each person was going through their own personal grief. Except for

Sabrina, this was everyone's first return, John realized, to the city each of them loved.

No longer angry at James, John stared out the window, allowing the sadness to overtake him, holding on to Sabrina's hand like a lifeline. He had always blocked off his thoughts about New Orleans because he didn't want to feel all that was lost. But now he had no choice. It was staring him in the face.

The blue roofs were the first thing he saw as they passed the cities west of New Orleans. He spotted hotels that looked as if giants had peeled away the outer layer before tossing things around inside. There was openness where walls should be. As they exited on Claiborne Avenue, the emptiness of the streets was the first thing that hit him.

There were no people.

Of course there were no people.

The houses they passed weren't fit for the roaches that thrived in the warm, moist climate of New Orleans. It was crazy for him to think about roaches, he knew, but his mind seemed stuck on the ludicrous question of whether they had survived. Finally tossing the thought aside, his eyes trained on the scene of destruction outside his window.

Despite the bright sunlight, houses stood hollow and dark, filthy because of the contaminated waters that had remained inside for weeks. Dark lines clearly marked the levels to which the water had invaded. Piles of debris sat on curbs, put there by those who had come home to begin cleanup.

Home.

This wasn't home.

Yet again, it was.

They passed through the Upper Ninth ward. Evidence of flooding and ruin was everywhere. He was ready to head back, he had seen enough. The bridge crossing the Industrial Canal loomed before them. The levee had broken somewhere near here. He remembered seeing the diagram in the newspaper. He had known it would be bad. Now he had no choice but to see.

The Ninth Ward was a town of decaying rubble where houses had once stood.

John stood.

Sabrina looked up at him, tears in her eyes, the same overwhelming hurt and sadness reflected in his own.

"Where's my trumpet?" he asked.

"Under your seat," she told him, releasing his hand and standing to let him reach under the seat.

"What are you up to, Red?" James asked. Everyone on the bus focused on John.

"It feels like a funeral in here."

"It is."

"Then why aren't we playing any dirges and hymns?" he asked, holding his trumpet and clicking the case closed.

"I don't know. Why don't you start us off?"

And he did.

The bus was soon filled with the sad, sorrowful tunes of loss and grief. John's soul vibrated through his trumpet. Lost in the music, he barely registered that a sax, trumpet and keyboard had joined in as they continued their ride through the Ninth Ward.

As they headed back toward the downtown area, they stopped at a site in the Upper Ninth Ward. James signaled for the band to stop playing. As the last painful note faded away, he announced. "This is the area where they're thinking of building the Musicians' Village. I don't know about you, but I like the idea of coming back to put some life into this city."

"That's right."

"You got it!"

Everyone else seemed to be able to respond to James's announcement with enthusiasm. John couldn't find it in himself.

"Grieving is over. Let's play!" James announced, leading them into the traditional raucous music that followed a jazz funeral, an indication that life does go on.

John found himself joining in halfheartedly, still disturbed by all he had seen, all he could still see as, they headed to Fat Harry's.

Experiencing the loss of her city through John's eyes was more painful than Sabrina's first visit a few weeks ago. But it was a necessary pain. Sabrina understood that John needed to face the hurt or it would eat him up. John was like those still waters that run deep. Sabrina was grateful to James for forcing John to face the facts. Still, she had the feeling that they were only treading water right now. The profound sadness that had poured from him as he played dirges and hymns surrounded him like a dense shield. And his heart wasn't in the celebration afterward. Even the session at Fat Harry's was not as heartfelt as usual.

Sabrina was worried about him.

The ride back to Baton Rouge after the gig was a silent one. He held her again but didn't say a word. He offered to drive back to Gonzales so she let him, thinking that concentrating on the road would keep him from dwelling on everything he'd seen.

She knew he had to talk about it. Had to get it all out. Tomorrow they would talk. It was Thanksgiving and the whole family would be together. Those who hadn't arrived yet would come. And she was looking forward to having Grammy and Uncle Darren there.

John would feel better surrounded by family. Then he'd be able to actually see that despite the pain of suffering and loss they had many things to be thankful for.

The next morning Sabrina awoke to the smell of a roasting turkey and the sounds of clanging pans and hushed voices. She found Miss Joyce, Monica, Ness and the other ladies hands deep in separating ingredients to take to the other houses to cook the fixings that would go with the turkey already baking in the oven.

"We didn't mean to wake you up," Miss Joyce said when Sabrina entered the kitchen. "We know you two got in pretty late last night."

"Yeah, the band played at Fat Harry's."

"Fat Harry's in New Orleans?" Monica asked.

Sabrina nodded.

"Was John up for that?" Ness asked.

"He didn't have much of a choice. Have you seen him this morning?"

"I don't think he's up yet. How did he take it?"

Their conversation was cut short by the arrival of their oldest brother Warren and his family. And Sabrina was relieved that it was. She didn't feel right discussing John's reaction with his family. He would need to do that himself. Sabrina greeted the new arrivals, then went in search of John, first peeking inside the room he was sharing with Josh. She saw no sign of either. After searching the house, the yard and the porch, she popped inside the houses on either side to see various courses of the meal being prepared but John was nowhere in sight. Coming back into the center house she found Warren, a man famous for his desserts, who with the help of his two kids, and a few of his nieces and nephews, was preparing to do magic with the enormous amount of baking goods spread all over the countertops. "Come and bake desserts with us, Sabrina," Vicki called out to her.

Since she couldn't find John, who probably needed to be left alone for a while anyway, she decided to stay and learn a thing or two from Warren. She dove right in, figuring Warren could use a hand managing his baking assistants.

"Thanks," he mouthed.

Three hours, four cakes, three pies and a chocolate mousse later, Sabrina directed cleanup of the kitchen declaring, "A good baker is a clean baker."

John popped in during "The Great Table Wiping Race" and gave her one of those strange looks before greeting Warren with a hearty embrace and a ton of conversation. Warren was another brother he hadn't seen since before the storm.

"Having fun?" he stepped over a few minutes later to ask, giving her a quick peck on the cheek before rushing off on some errand for his dad, not bothering to ask if she wanted to come. It could have been because Warren was joining him so she tried not to take offense.

As the morning wore on more relatives joined the gathering. Grammy and Uncle Darren arrived not long after. Sabrina was taking it all in, having the time of her life. She went from one house to the other, seeing what needed to be done, being stopped on more than one occasion, by a child or an adult, to share a word or lend a helping hand. She would spot John once in a while but there never seemed to be a moment when she could pull him to the side just to have a word with him to assure herself that he was all right. He seemed to be okay. There was a sadness that lingered in his eyes but that was to be expected.

In the dining room, under the direction of their dad, Josh and John had set up three long tables in the shape of a boxy U. Sabrina loved the fact that the kids weren't sent off to the side and that everyone ate together.

By two o'clock, a ton of food sat on the table, children were secured in highchairs, and everyone was assigned a seat, hers to the right of John. Calvin Lewis, the head of this beautiful, loving family stood. "Are we thankful?" he bellowed.

"Yes," all the kids yelled, used to their grandfather's unusual antics.

"I heard the kids," he said in a much softer voice. "But how about the rest of you? Are you thankful?"

"Yes."

"Of course."

"You know it, Dad."

"Well, I'm thankful that that windy girl Katrina didn't take any of you away. I'm thankful that you're all here with me, alive and well. Others weren't so lucky. I know that you all are thankful for that, too."

There were several nods and a few verbal responses.

"But there are other things to be thankful for. Everyone of you needs to say what you're thankful for. I don't want all forty something of you to stand here and announce it for all to hear. No, that would take forever, and I don't know about you but I'm starving."

Forty-something kids and adults laughed.

"What I want you to do is to take a minute right now where you are, think about exactly what it is that you are thankful for. Say it out loud, whisper it, or keep it in your heart, but acknowledge the things you are thankful for today, family."

When all remained quiet he added, "What are you waiting for? Start thanking!"

Sabrina watched as little ones closed their eyes whispering their thanks. Couples leaned into one another to whisper or hung their heads in deep thought. From across the table Sabrina saw Darren's lips move. "Diane," they said. Grammy was quiet, her head bowed, so Sabrina had no idea what Grammy was thankful for.

"You." The word eased into her ear in a soft, warm breath.

Sabrina looked up at John.

"I'm thankful for you," he told her.

"And I for you," she said seconds before Mr. Calvin bellowed, "Let's eat!"

And they did, teasing and laughing as the food began to disappear. Declarations of being stuffed soon filled the room until Warren and his baking assistants announced dessert. Suddenly everyone had room for dessert. When everyone had been served and was absorbed in satisfying their taste buds, Josh inadvertently brought up their visit to New Orleans.

"John, I went to that club in Baton Rouge where you told me you were playing but The Jazz wasn't there. There was some techno group playing."

"Sorry about that. I was misled."

"What happened? Where'd ya'll play?"

"In New Orleans at Fat Harry's."

"You went into the city?"

"Like you suggested."

"Like I told you you needed to do."

Josh and John had obviously had a conversation that she didn't know anything about, Sabrina surmised, looking from one to the other.

"I didn't exactly have any choice. I had to be there. It's my job."

"How'd it go?" Josh asked.

"I don't want to talk about it."

Sabrina started to get an uncomfortable feeling. The issue that Josh was bringing up was the exact issue she had wanted to speak to John about, but in private, not in front of his whole family. At least they were sitting at the far end of the dining table and no one else seemed to notice the content of the conversation, but she felt as if she were smack in the middle of something and had no idea where it was heading.

"So, you had to be there, huh? What you need to be is glad you're alive to be able to talk about it. Are you planning to help out with the Musicians' Village?"

"The Musicians' Village? I heard about that." Miss Joyce had come over to set a piece of pumpkin pie in front of each of them. Her hand landed on John's shoulder for just a moment. Did she suspect what was going on? Could she feel the tension on this side of the room? Sabrina certainly could.

"Oh yeah," Ness said from across the room. "Habitat for Humanity is teaming up with a group organized by Harry Connick, Jr, and Branford Marsalis."

"Wasn't there something you e-mailed me about? A concert at Tipitina's and an interview with Michael White, the clarinetist who works at Xavier University."

"I read that article and saw a video streaming of the interview," Sabrina said to anyone within hearing distance, attempting to make it a casual comment. "I e-mailed it to John. We even passed the area where they're thinking about building the Musicians' Village," Sabrina answered, desperately wanting to stop the stem of questions.

John looked at her as if she had betrayed him by adding this bit of information, though she hadn't said anything wrong or mentioned anything about how he had personally reacted.

"Tell us what you know about it," Warren requested.

"John, will you help to build some of the houses?" Scott asked. "You've got the know-how, brother-in-law.

"We taught him everything he knows," Devin added.

"The Ninth Ward's not my district, and even though I've been working twelve-hour shifts I heard about it, too." Randy walked over, a slice of pie in his hand. "So, little brother," he said after he swallowed a bite, "fill us in on what's going on. How many houses are they building? Exactly where will the village be located? What kind of houses? What are you going to do to help?"

Randy's questions seem to flow out one after the other without pause. Sabrina wondered if he specialized in investigation because he was definitely trying to get as much information out of John as he could, having no idea that he was causing his brother more pain.

"Enough with the questions. I don't know and I don't care. If you want information, ask Sabrina. She'll be more than happy to tell you, going so far as looking up the information if it means she gets to hang around any of my family a few minutes longer."

There was complete silence as everyone stared at John in disbelief. His reaction was so uncharacteristic that everyone was stunned into silence; everyone except his mom.

"John, that was rude," Miss Joyce told her son.

"Yes, it was," he said, looking directly at Sabrina.

Joyce Lewis walked over to John. Sabrina watched as she leaned down to say to her son, just loud enough for the both of them to hear, "Take Sabrina outside and handle your business," she suggested.

Never taking his eyes off her, he stood without a word, reached a hand down and said, "Come on, Riff."

If his tone hadn't held a promise of an apology and if he hadn't called her Riff, Sabrina knew that she would have sat exactly where she was until she was ready to take care of business.

"What was that about?" she asked as soon as they reached the end of the driveway.

"It was about me trying to deal with the pressure of my family expecting me to do what I always do the way I always do it. Sabrina, they expect me to jump in to help. I always help. It's what I do. It's part of being John Lewis. But I can't help. Not when I feel so angry about all this."

"That I understand. You talking to me about how you feel is what I've wanted. It's what you need. You are who you are, and you will get to a point where you are no longer angry and you will be yourself. Let me help you make this better."

"How?"

"You know I'm heading back to Lafayette today."

"Yes."

"Tomorrow, Uncle Darren and I will be taking Grammy to see the house. Come with us tomorrow."

"I don't think so. See it all again twice in one week? No way. We'll be touring in Louisiana and I'll be close enough to home to get there when I'm ready."

"And when will you be ready? You weren't ready to go yesterday, but you did and handled yourself. Come again. This time will be easier."

"How can you know what would be easier for me?"

"Because I know you."

"If you know me, Sabrina, then you know that you're pushing too hard. I had enough pushing from my family just now."

"You're right. I won't push, but I'll be there if you change your mind."

"I won't."

"We've had dinner and dessert. I think it's time my family and I left you to your family."

"I'm sorry about that. My mother was right. That was rude."

"That crack you said about me and your family? Yes, John that was rude. What was *that* all about?"

"My big mouth bursting with something I've been wondering about."

"What?"

"You love my family."

"Was that a question? Yes, and . . ."

"Why do you love them?"

"Because they're a great bunch of people. Should I hate them instead? Is that what you want?"

"Of course not. What I need to know is . . . Are you with me so that you can be a part of my family?"

"That's ridiculous."

"If it's so ridiculous then why is it so easy to say you love them when you've never said those words to me."

Sabrina simply stared at him. He could not be so dense. But then again, thinking about the winding path they'd taken to get even this far, he could. "I'll let you figure that one out on your own," she told him, deciding it really was time to go.

In a matter of ten minutes Sabrina had left, barely giving him enough time to wrap his brain around all that had happened in the last hour. He had been sure of how he felt for her even though he had begun to wonder about how she felt for him. When his dad had made his Thanksgiving speech and John had whispered, "You," he had merely cut off the first two words of "I love you." He'd wanted to tell her. Had felt it since their wine and cheese cracker picnic. John had planned on telling her today, but that was before.

Before Josh's comment reinforced in his mind the idea that Sabrina didn't want him for himself. The idea that she might have gone after him as a way to be part of his family sounded too much like the groupie thing all over again.

Before his mind and conscience were bombarded with scenes of Katrina's aftermath and his responsibility as a citizen of New Orleans.

It was a good thing that she'd left. He was as about ready to say that he loved her as he was ready to go back into the city.

John went back into the house and pretended to watch the football game. He focused enough to give Grammy a kiss good-bye and respond to Sabrina's uncle when he told him, "Don't let it go too long. Silence can create more problems."

John saw them out, but returned to his seat a few minutes later, nodding when somebody talked to him, and eventually going to his room long before the day was over. He was thankful that his family knew when to stop asking questions.

He prowled the room, not wanting to leave but frustrated with standing still. He went to Josh's laptop, turned it on to check his e-mail and what should he find but a letter from Sabrina? He opened it. It was the video interview with Michael White. John sat through the interview, learning more about how other musicians were handling their situations. They were handling their business. He needed to handle his. He knew this. The interview took him from Tipitina's, a local jazz bar that had just opened starring many displaced musicians, to Michael White's home that had had up to nine feet of water in it. He had lost not only his home but some jazz history. Artifacts and scores he had written had been destroyed by the floodwaters. But he was back.

The last segment of the interview struck a cord with him. Michael White compared what New Orleans was going through with a jazz funeral. Sorrow and grieving were represented by dirges and hymns but after the burial there was a celebration of living and life. What Michael White talked about was exactly what John had tried to create on the bus. But his sorrow had been too deep to allow him to celebrate. He needed to get it all out.

John grabbed his trumpet, asked Devin to borrow his truck, and drove out to the middle of nowhere.

He sat in the bed of the truck and played. He played dirges and every hymn he could think of until he couldn't blow a second more. He played out his sorrow and his anger. Putting the trumpet back into its case, he lay on his back in the bed of the truck. A few thoughts popped inside his head as a few stars appeared in the night sky.

He had not allowed himself to feel the pain so he could not truly grieve his loss.

Sabrina knew that. She knew him because she truly loved him.

Heart soaring, he hopped into the cab and drove back to his family. Going to the door of the center house, he called out, "Second line!" and began to play.

Just as he knew they would, every member of his family, young and old, came out and he and his trumpet led in the procession with everyone else following and waving napkins and towels in celebration and *thanksgiving.*

CHAPTER 15

Grammy stood at the door of her home for the first time since she'd evacuated late last August. A deep inward breath lifted her shoulders, the only reaction Sabrina could see.

Grammy was silent and had been that way since the scenery had changed from the highway surrounded by nature to the highway surrounded by destruction.

Silently is how she moved through each and every room, the periodic intake of breath the only assurance she and Darren had that she was finding a way to cope with the loss of a life she had held dear.

Silently she walked out of the house, down the path and straight to Darren's truck where she stopped and turned.

Sabrina followed her and as soon as she reached her side Grammy told her, "I don't want it. It's all yours, Sabrina. I'm staying in Lafayette." A sadness surrounded Grammy as the words flowed past her lips.

"Are you sure, Grammy?" Sabrina watched a fortified breath fill Grammy, then saw resolve and renewed strength suddenly blaze in her eyes.

"I'm sure. We've got it all worked out. Faith and I will be moving into Diane's house. Diane will be moving in with Darren. After they're married, of course."

"Of course," Uncle Darren readily agreed.

"Then I'll be expecting some more grandbabies. Let's get going," Grammy said to her son as he guided her past some debris that hadn't been picked up yet.

"Give me a minute," Sabrina said, turning to face the bare-bones structure again. She could rebuild, even have the house elevated. She wanted to become a part of helping New Orleans come alive again.

"You may need a couple of minutes," Grammy called through the window of Darren's truck.

"What?" Then she spotted John as he spoke to her uncle.

"We'll see you at home," Grammy called as they drove away.

"Now why would they think that I wanted to be left with you?" She grinned up at him, catching a glimpse of the John she knew before Katrina had torn him up inside.

"Because I told them I had something very important to tell you."

"And that would be?"

He hesitated, took a deep breath and said, "I love you."

"Oh." Her heart jumped inside her throat.

"Do you have any idea how often you say that?"

"No idea."

"I'm taking that 'oh' to mean that you're pleasantly surprised that I've figured things out."

"You can take it that way."

"You see, I also know that you love me."

"You do?"

"Even more than my family."

"How do you figure that?"

"Because everything you do tells me that. I couldn't see it because I've got this tendency to hold onto things."

"Such as?"

"My image of you as a child."

"Long gone."

"My fear of coping with it all."

"You're doing that by being here today. We all have our own way of grieving."

"Well, my grieving process caused me to lose a few things. I went to my home. The landlord had everything cleared away. He told me he'd tried to get in touch with me. I can remember ignoring his calls."

"But you came, that's all that's important. Those were just things."

"So I told myself. There's something else I held on to."

"What was that?"

"You. I held onto you so tightly I couldn't see the love you have for me. I'm saying it again. I love you, Sabrina." His hands at her waist, he pulled her toward him to kiss her, stopping before deepening the kiss to hold her face in his palms. "I love you."

"I knew that. I've always known that."

"That's because you *do* know me. Know me so well, it's scary. I bet you can tell what I'm thinking now."

"Let's get out of here so that you can show me how much you love me."

"Exactly."

"What do you have in mind?"

"Think of this. A moonlit night, wine and cheese crackers, and a man with the woman he loves and his trumpet."

Sabrina had to wait a few hours until she discovered what it all meant. At dusk, they reached a secluded field, far from the lights of the city and watchful eyes of family. He spread a blanket in the bed of the truck and laid out their lovers' feast of wine and cheese crackers.

"Tradition," she said as John plied her with food and drink, eased her onto the blanket and proceeded to make her body hum with need for him. His fingers outlined her breasts, never truly touching her, merely making her anticipate his touch. He skimmed her thighs and the apex between them with a flutter of a touch that had her almost screaming with want.

"I have something for you," he whispered, his hands making a path between her breasts.

"Hands, lips and a tongue that actually touch me where I want to be touched?"

"Soon."

"Now."

"Come here, Riff. We have to do this first."

"Okay," she sighed as she reluctantly sat up. John went inside the cab of the truck and came back playing his trumpet. He was playing a song she had never heard before, its deep, soulful rhythm making her sway, her eyes closed, as she imagined John's hands on her breasts and traveling down her body.

The trumpet stopped as he sang, "Saaaabriiiinaaa, Sabrina, Sabrina, Sabrina. Marry, marry, marry, marry me," he sang, two, three, four times. He saw the answer in her eyes as the trumpet returned to his lips to release the final notes of a song that told her that she had captured his heart.

Dropping his trumpet to the ground, John hopped into the bed of the truck, softly landing beside her, his arms outstretched. Sabrina lean into him, the vibrations from his beautiful riff tune humming beneath her skin, escalating to a thunderous roar as his hands skimmed her down her arms, grazing her elbow before turning her toward him.

"Where do you want me to touch you, Riff?"

"Everywhere," she whispered.

And he did.

EPILOGUE

It was official. The construction on the Musicians' Village would begin. A live performance at the site in the Upper Ninth Ward celebrated the momentous occasion.

The Jazz joined several other popular bands in celebrating the new beginning. After the live performance Sabrina walked among politicians and celebrities, her eyes searching for the most important celebrity in her life. She spotted John talking to Michael White. Sabrina knew that it was Michael who'd inspired John to have his cake and eat it, too. John had plans to combine his teaching and musical careers just as Michael had managed to do. John wanted to go back to teaching kids about jazz so that the legacy could live on.

"Here's my wife," John said, introducing Sabrina to the famous clarinetist.

They had gotten married in a small church in Lafayette a week ago. They were living in a small apartment in Lafayette until the end of the school year so that Sabrina could finish the year out. John was working gigs closer to home, limiting the amount of separation they had to deal with. They'd already found jobs back in New Orleans for the next school year and planned on living in a FEMA trailer until they completed the rebuilding of the house Grammy had given them.

"Ready?" he asked her after sharing a few pleasantries with other members of the community.

"Yes." She grinned up at his ridiculous question. Mere minutes before they had left the apartment to drive into New Orleans John had cornered her in the kitchen, rubbed his body against her, half undressed her as his fingers caressed her breasts and shoulders, only to tell her that it was time for them to go. Ever since that moment she had been ready. The entire drive to New Orleans she had been ready. He had tuned her body and left it humming. The feeling was too reminiscent of the entire time they had dated and even to the weeks before they had gotten married.

It had been John's suggestion that they wait to make love until they got married. "We've waited all this time, we might as well wait until we're married," John had told her that night in the truck after proposing to her with that beautiful riff tune.

"Nice meeting you," Michael White said, bringing her mind back to the present.

They said their goodbyes, walked to their car and settled into their seats. "Where are we off to now?" John asked, a hand grazing her knee, knowing exactly what was on her mind.

"The house. We can stop to check on the progress before heading back to Lafayette."

"Check on the progress, huh?"

"Yep, I'm hoping to see some walls."

"Any particular reason?"

"I was just thinking that our future house would be a good place to finish what you started this morning."

"You mean you can't wait to have my body until we get to Lafayette?" he asked.

"You'll be lucky if I wait until we get to the house," she grinned at him.

John leaned over to kiss the lopsided grin off her face. "To the house then. I sure hope those walls are up and the floors aren't ice cold. If so, it'll be a sacrifice I'll have to endure to give my wife what she wants."

"Exactly." Sabrina grinned up at her husband.

When they got inside the house Sabrina was surprised to find a blanket, a bottle of wine in a tub, and cheese crackers in the middle of the living room.

"How?"

"Randy. Having a big family can be beneficial."

"Yes, it can."

Besides, we can't mess with tradition," he said, proceeding to remove her clothes. The dress she wore dropped to the floor with a simple easing of the zipper. John's hands skimmed the soft skin of her shoulders, gliding down her back to cup her bottom. Sabrina didn't let him get away with the slow, easy pace he was setting. She was making fast work of getting rid of his clothes.

John knew what he had done to her before leaving the house. He had done it to himself, too. Hours spent imagining her skin beneath his touch, her firm breasts in his hands. Thinking of them, his hands found their softness, his thumbs grazing her nipples standing tall and ready. He was ready, which Sabrina discovered as she slid his pants down his legs, her entire body taking part in the movement so that he lost the feel of her breasts in his hands only to enjoy their heated caress down his body as she moved against him like an erotic dancer.

"Come here, John. Help me warm this blanket."

John didn't need more prompting. He was with her, had been with her for the last month and a half. Sabrina was the music of his life. She rolled onto her back, pulling him down toward her. He moved into her and with her, the music flowing between them, riff tunes of satisfaction tearing from his soul as he made love to her.

Much later, Sabrina sighed as she snuggled into her husband. "Now I can deal with a two hour drive back to Lafayette."

"Not too soon, I hope."

"Not too soon," she agreed.

"We've got wine and crackers to eat and work off."

"That could take hours."

"I've got hours," John said. "How about you?"

"For you, I've got a lifetime, John Lewis."

"Same here, Mrs. Lewis. You are my shelter in the storm."

ABOUT THE AUTHOR

Pamela Leigh Starr, a wife and mother of three children, works to aid teachers in creating readers and, hopefully, future fans in her occupation as a staff trainer for an educational publishing company. Ms. Starr traces the beginning of her love for writing back to her very first creation entitled, *The Terrifying Night,* which was a twenty page comedic thriller illustrated by a fellow 7th grade classmate. Long after this first attempt, Ms. Starr found the courage to develop love stories that were both thrilling and romantic, and she continues to do just this. She has fallen in love with presenting the never-ending cycle of two people who meet, open their hearts and then find their way to love.

2008 Reprint Mass Market Titles

January

Cautious Heart
Cheris F. Hodges
ISBN-13: 978-1-58571-301-1
ISBN-10: 1-58571-301-5
$6.99

Suddenly You
Crystal Hubbard
ISBN-13: 978-1-58571-302-8
ISBN-10: 1-58571-302-3
$6.99

February

Passion
T. T. Henderson
ISBN-13: 978-1-58571-303-5
ISBN-10: 1-58571-303-1
$6.99

Whispers in the Sand
LaFlorya Gauthier
ISBN-13: 978-1-58571-304-2
ISBN-10: 1-58571-304-x
$6.99

March

Life Is Never As It Seems
J. J. Michael
ISBN-13: 978-1-58571-305-9
ISBN-10: 1-58571-305-8
$6.99

Beyond the Rapture
Beverly Clark
ISBN-13: 978-1-58571-306-6
ISBN-10: 1-58571-306-6
$6.99

April

A Heart's Awakening
Veronica Parker
ISBN-13: 978-1-58571-307-3
ISBN-10: 1-58571-307-4
$6.99

Breeze
Robin Lynette Hampton
ISBN-13: 978-1-58571-308-0
ISBN-10: 1-58571-308-2
$6.99

May

I'll Be Your Shelter
Giselle Carmichael
ISBN-13: 978-1-58571-309-7
ISBN-10: 1-58571-309-0
$6.99

Careless Whispers
Rochelle Alers
ISBN-13: 978-1-58571-310-3
ISBN-10: 1-58571-310-4
$6.99

June

Sin
Crystal Rhodes
ISBN-13: 978-1-58571-311-0
ISBN-10: 1-58571-311-2
$6.99

Dark Storm Rising
Chinelu Moore
ISBN-13: 978-1-58571-312-7
ISBN-10: 1-58571-312-0
$6.99

2008 Reprint Mass Market Titles (continued)

July

Object of His Desire
A.C. Arthur
ISBN-13: 978-1-58571-313-4
ISBN-10: 1-58571-313-9
$6.99

Angel's Paradise
Janice Angelique
ISBN-13: 978-1-58571-314-1
ISBN-10: 1-58571-314-7
$6.99

August

Unbreak My Heart
Dar Tomlinson
ISBN-13: 978-1-58571-315-8
ISBN-10: 1-58571-315-5
$6.99

All I Ask
Barbara Keaton
ISBN-13: 978-1-58571-316-5
ISBN-10: 1-58571-316-3
$6.99

September

Icie
Pamela Leigh Starr
ISBN-13: 978-1-58571-275-5
ISBN-10: 1-58571-275-2
$6.99

At Last
Lisa Riley
ISBN-13: 978-1-58571-276-2
ISBN-10: 1-58571-276-0
$6.99

October

Everlastin' Love
Gay G. Gunn
ISBN-13: 978-1-58571-277-9
ISBN-10: 1-58571-277-9
$6.99

Three Wishes
Seressia Glass
ISBN-13: 978-1-58571-278-6
ISBN-10: 1-58571-278-7
$6.99

November

Yesterday Is Gone
Beverly Clark
ISBN-13: 978-1-58571-279-3
ISBN-10: 1-58571-279-5
$6.99

Again My Love
Kayla Perrin
ISBN-13: 978-1-58571-280-9
ISBN-10: 1-58571-280-9
$6.99

December

Office Policy
A.C. Arthur
ISBN-13: 978-1-58571-281-6
ISBN-10: 1-58571-281-7
$6.99

Rendezvous With Fate
Jeanne Sumerix
ISBN-13: 978-1-58571-283-3
ISBN-10: 1-58571-283-3
$6.99

2008 New Mass Market Titles

January

Where I Want To Be
Maryam Diaab
ISBN-13: 978-1-58571-268-7
ISBN-10: 1-58571-268-X
$6.99

Never Say Never
Michele Cameron
ISBN-13: 978-1-58571-269-4
ISBN-10: 1-58571-269-8
$6.99

February

Stolen Memories
Michele Sudler
ISBN-13: 978-1-58571-270-0
ISBN-10: 1-58571-270-1
$6.99

Dawn's Harbor
Kymberly Hunt
ISBN-13: 978-1-58571-271-7
ISBN-10: 1-58571-271-X
$6.99

March

Undying Love
Renee Alexis
ISBN-13: 978-1-58571-272-4
ISBN-10: 1-58571-272-8
$6.99

Blame It On Paradise
Crystal Hubbard
ISBN-13: 978-1-58571-273-1
ISBN-10: 1-58571-273-6
$6.99

April

When A Man Loves A Woman
La Connie Taylor-Jones
ISBN-13: 978-1-58571-274-8
ISBN-10: 1-58571-274-4
$6.99

Choices
Tammy Williams
ISBN-13: 978-1-58571-300-4
ISBN-10: 1-58571-300-7
$6.99

May

Dream Runner
Gail McFarland
ISBN-13: 978-1-58571-317-2
ISBN-10: 1-58571-317-1
$6.99

Southern Fried Standards
S.R. Maddox
ISBN-13: 978-1-58571-318-9
ISBN-10: 1-58571-318-X
$6.99

June

Looking for Lily
Africa Fine
ISBN-13: 978-1-58571-319-6
ISBN-10: 1-58571-319-8
$6.99

Bliss, Inc.
Chamein Canton
ISBN-13: 978-1-58571-325-7
ISBN-10: 1-58571-325-2
$6.99

2008 New Mass Market Titles (continued)

July

Love's Secrets
Yolanda McVey
ISBN-13: 978-1-58571-321-9
ISBN-10: 1-58571-321-X
$6.99

Things Forbidden
Maryam Diaab
ISBN-13: 978-1-58571-327-1
ISBN-10: 1-58571-327-9
$6.99

August

Storm
Pamela Leigh Starr
ISBN-13: 978-1-58571-323-3
ISBN-10: 1-58571-323-6
$6.99

Passion's Furies
AlTonya Washington
ISBN-13: 978-1-58571-324-0
ISBN-10: 1-58571-324-4
$6.99

September

Three Doors Down
Michele Sudler
ISBN-13: 978-1-58571-332-5
ISBN-10: 1-58571-332-5
$6.99

Mr Fix-It
Crystal Hubbard
ISBN-13: 978-1-58571-326-4
ISBN-10: 1-58571-326-0
$6.99

October

Moments of Clarity
Michele Cameron
ISBN-13: 978-1-58571-330-1
ISBN-10: 1-58571-330-9
$6.99

Lady Preacher
K.T. Richey
ISBN-13: 978-1-58571-333-2
ISBN-10: 1-58571-333-3
$6.99

November

This Life Isn't Perfect Holla
Sandra Foy
ISBN: 978-1-58571-331-8
ISBN-10: 1-58571-331-7
$6.99

Promises Made
Bernice Layton
ISBN-13: 978-1-58571-334-9
ISBN-10: 1-58571-334-1
$6.99

December

A Voice Behind Thunder
Carrie Elizabeth Greene
ISBN-13: 978-1-58571-329-5
ISBN-10: 1-58571-329-5
$6.99

The More Things Change
Chamein Canton
ISBN-13: 978-1-58571-328-8
ISBN-10: 1-58571-328-7
$6.99

Other Genesis Press, Inc. Titles

Other Genesis Press, Inc. Titles (continued)

Blaze	Barbara Keaton	$9.95
Blood Lust	J. M. Jeffries	$9.95
Blood Seduction	J.M. Jeffries	$9.95
Bodyguard	Andrea Jackson	$9.95
Boss of Me	Diana Nyad	$8.95
Bound by Love	Beverly Clark	$8.95
Breeze	Robin Hampton Allen	$10.95
Broken	Dar Tomlinson	$24.95
By Design	Barbara Keaton	$8.95
Cajun Heat	Charlene Berry	$8.95
Careless Whispers	Rochelle Alers	$8.95
Cats & Other Tales	Marilyn Wagner	$8.95
Caught in a Trap	Andre Michelle	$8.95
Caught Up In the Rapture	Lisa G. Riley	$9.95
Cautious Heart	Cheris F Hodges	$8.95
Chances	Pamela Leigh Starr	$8.95
Cherish the Flame	Beverly Clark	$8.95
Class Reunion	Irma Jenkins/ John Brown	$12.95
Code Name: Diva	J.M. Jeffries	$9.95
Conquering Dr. Wexler's Heart	Kimberley White	$9.95
Corporate Seduction	A.C. Arthur	$9.95
Crossing Paths, Tempting Memories	Dorothy Elizabeth Love	$9.95
Crush	Crystal Hubbard	$9.95
Cypress Whisperings	Phyllis Hamilton	$8.95
Dark Embrace	Crystal Wilson Harris	$8.95
Dark Storm Rising	Chinelu Moore	$10.95

Other Genesis Press, Inc. Titles (continued)

Daughter of the Wind	Joan Xian	$8.95
Deadly Sacrifice	Jack Kean	$22.95
Designer Passion	Dar Tomlinson Diana Richeaux	$8.95
Do Over	Celya Bowers	$9.95
Dreamtective	Liz Swados	$5.95
Ebony Angel	Deatri King-Bey	$9.95
Ebony Butterfly II	Delilah Dawson	$14.95
Echoes of Yesterday	Beverly Clark	$9.95
Eden's Garden	Elizabeth Rose	$8.95
Eve's Prescription	Edwina Martin Arnold	$8.95
Everlastin' Love	Gay G. Gunn	$8.95
Everlasting Moments	Dorothy Elizabeth Love	$8.95
Everything and More	Sinclair Lebeau	$8.95
Everything but Love	Natalie Dunbar	$8.95
Falling	Natalie Dunbar	$9.95
Fate	Pamela Leigh Starr	$8.95
Finding Isabella	A.J. Garrotto	$8.95
Forbidden Quest	Dar Tomlinson	$10.95
Forever Love	Wanda Y. Thomas	$8.95
From the Ashes	Kathleen Suzanne Jeanne Sumerix	$8.95
Gentle Yearning	Rochelle Alers	$10.95
Glory of Love	Sinclair LeBeau	$10.95
Go Gentle into that Good Night	Malcom Boyd	$12.95
Goldengroove	Mary Beth Craft	$16.95
Groove, Bang, and Jive	Steve Cannon	$8.99
Hand in Glove	Andrea Jackson	$9.95

Other Genesis Press, Inc. Titles (continued)

Hard to Love	Kimberley White	$9.95
Hart & Soul	Angie Daniels	$8.95
Heart of the Phoenix	A.C. Arthur	$9.95
Heartbeat	Stephanie Bedwell-Grime	$8.95
Hearts Remember	M. Loui Quezada	$8.95
Hidden Memories	Robin Allen	$10.95
Higher Ground	Leah Latimer	$19.95
Hitler, the War, and the Pope	Ronald Rychiak	$26.95
How to Write a Romance	Kathryn Falk	$18.95
I Married a Reclining Chair	Lisa M. Fuhs	$8.95
I'll Be Your Shelter	Giselle Carmichael	$8.95
I'll Paint a Sun	A.J. Garrotto	$9.95
Icie	Pamela Leigh Starr	$8.95
Illusions	Pamela Leigh Starr	$8.95
Indigo After Dark Vol. I	Nia Dixon/Angelique	$10.95
Indigo After Dark Vol. II	Dolores Bundy/ Cole Riley	$10.95
Indigo After Dark Vol. III	Montana Blue/ Coco Morena	$10.95
Indigo After Dark Vol. IV	Cassandra Colt/	$14.95
Indigo After Dark Vol. V	Delilah Dawson	$14.95
Indiscretions	Donna Hill	$8.95
Intentional Mistakes	Michele Sudler	$9.95
Interlude	Donna Hill	$8.95
Intimate Intentions	Angie Daniels	$8.95
It's Not Over Yet	J.J. Michael	$9.95
Jolie's Surrender	Edwina Martin-Arnold	$8.95
Kiss or Keep	Debra Phillips	$8.95
Lace	Giselle Carmichael	$9.95

Other Genesis Press, Inc. Titles (continued)

Last Train to Memphis	Elsa Cook	$12.95
Lasting Valor	Ken Olsen	$24.95
Let Us Prey	Hunter Lundy	$25.95
Lies Too Long	Pamela Ridley	$13.95
Life Is Never As It Seems	J.J. Michael	$12.95
Lighter Shade of Brown	Vicki Andrews	$8.95
Love Always	Mildred E. Riley	$10.95
Love Doesn't Come Easy	Charlyne Dickerson	$8.95
Love Unveiled	Gloria Greene	$10.95
Love's Deception	Charlene Berry	$10.95
Love's Destiny	M. Loui Quezada	$8.95
Mae's Promise	Melody Walcott	$8.95
Magnolia Sunset	Giselle Carmichael	$8.95
Many Shades of Gray	Dyanne Davis	$6.99
Matters of Life and Death	Lesego Malepe, Ph.D.	$15.95
Meant to Be	Jeanne Sumerix	$8.95
Midnight Clear (Anthology)	Leslie Esdaile Gwynne Forster Carmen Green Monica Jackson	$10.95
Midnight Magic	Gwynne Forster	$8.95
Midnight Peril	Vicki Andrews	$10.95
Misconceptions	Pamela Leigh Starr	$9.95
Montgomery's Children	Richard Perry	$14.95
My Buffalo Soldier	Barbara B. K. Reeves	$8.95
Naked Soul	Gwynne Forster	$8.95
Next to Last Chance	Louisa Dixon	$24.95
No Apologies	Seressia Glass	$8.95
No Commitment Required	Seressia Glass	$8.95

Other Genesis Press, Inc. Titles (continued)

No Regrets	Mildred E. Riley	$8.95
Not His Type	Chamein Canton	$6.99
Nowhere to Run	Gay G. Gunn	$10.95
O Bed! O Breakfast!	Rob Kuehnle	$14.95
Object of His Desire	A. C. Arthur	$8.95
Office Policy	A. C. Arthur	$9.95
Once in a Blue Moon	Dorianne Cole	$9.95
One Day at a Time	Bella McFarland	$8.95
One in A Million	Barbara Keaton	$6.99
One of These Days	Michele Sudler	$9.95
Outside Chance	Louisa Dixon	$24.95
Passion	T.T. Henderson	$10.95
Passion's Blood	Cherif Fortin	$22.95
Passion's Journey	Wanda Y. Thomas	$8.95
Past Promises	Jahmel West	$8.95
Path of Fire	T.T. Henderson	$8.95
Path of Thorns	Annetta P. Lee	$9.95
Peace Be Still	Colette Haywood	$12.95
Picture Perfect	Reon Carter	$8.95
Playing for Keeps	Stephanie Salinas	$8.95
Pride & Joi	Gay G. Gunn	$15.95
Pride & Joi	Gay G. Gunn	$8.95
Promises to Keep	Alicia Wiggins	$8.95
Quiet Storm	Donna Hill	$10.95
Reckless Surrender	Rochelle Alers	$6.95
Red Polka Dot in a World of Plaid	Varian Johnson	$12.95
Reluctant Captive	Joyce Jackson	$8.95
Rendezvous with Fate	Jeanne Sumerix	$8.95

Other Genesis Press, Inc. Titles (continued)

Revelations	Cheris F. Hodges	$8.95
Rivers of the Soul	Leslie Esdaile	$8.95
Rocky Mountain Romance	Kathleen Suzanne	$8.95
Rooms of the Heart	Donna Hill	$8.95
Rough on Rats and Tough on Cats	Chris Parker	$12.95
Secret Library Vol. 1	Nina Sheridan	$18.95
Secret Library Vol. 2	Cassandra Colt	$8.95
Secret Thunder	Annetta P. Lee	$9.95
Shades of Brown	Denise Becker	$8.95
Shades of Desire	Monica White	$8.95
Shadows in the Moonlight	Jeanne Sumerix	$8.95
Sin	Crystal Rhodes	$8.95
Small Whispers	Annetta P. Lee	$6.99
So Amazing	Sinclair LeBeau	$8.95
Somebody's Someone	Sinclair LeBeau	$8.95
Someone to Love	Alicia Wiggins	$8.95
Song in the Park	Martin Brant	$15.95
Soul Eyes	Wayne L. Wilson	$12.95
Soul to Soul	Donna Hill	$8.95
Southern Comfort	J.M. Jeffries	$8.95
Still the Storm	Sharon Robinson	$8.95
Still Waters Run Deep	Leslie Esdaile	$8.95
Stolen Kisses	Dominiqua Douglas	$9.95
Stories to Excite You	Anna Forrest/Divine	$14.95
Subtle Secrets	Wanda Y. Thomas	$8.95
Suddenly You	Crystal Hubbard	$9.95
Sweet Repercussions	Kimberley White	$9.95
Sweet Sensations	Gwendolyn Bolton	$9.95

Other Genesis Press, Inc. Titles (continued)

Sweet Tomorrows	Kimberly White	$8.95
Taken by You	Dorothy Elizabeth Love	$9.95
Tattooed Tears	T. T. Henderson	$8.95
The Color Line	Lizzette Grayson Carter	$9.95
The Color of Trouble	Dyanne Davis	$8.95
The Disappearance of Allison Jones	Kayla Perrin	$5.95
The Fires Within	Beverly Clark	$9.95
The Foursome	Celya Bowers	$6.99
The Honey Dipper's Legacy	Pannell-Allen	$14.95
The Joker's Love Tune	Sidney Rickman	$15.95
The Little Pretender	Barbara Cartland	$10.95
The Love We Had	Natalie Dunbar	$8.95
The Man Who Could Fly	Bob & Milana Beamon	$18.95
The Missing Link	Charlyne Dickerson	$8.95
The Mission	Pamela Leigh Starr	$6.99
The Perfect Frame	Beverly Clark	$9.95
The Price of Love	Sinclair LeBeau	$8.95
The Smoking Life	Ilene Barth	$29.95
The Words of the Pitcher	Kei Swanson	$8.95
Three Wishes	Seressia Glass	$8.95
Ties That Bind	Kathleen Suzanne	$8.95
Tiger Woods	Libby Hughes	$5.95
Time is of the Essence	Angie Daniels	$9.95
Timeless Devotion	Bella McFarland	$9.95
Tomorrow's Promise	Leslie Esdaile	$8.95
Truly Inseparable	Wanda Y. Thomas	$8.95
Two Sides to Every Story	Dyanne Davis	$9.95
Unbreak My Heart	Dar Tomlinson	$8.95

Other Genesis Press, Inc. Titles (continued)

Uncommon Prayer	Kenneth Swanson	$9.95
Unconditional Love	Alicia Wiggins	$8.95
Unconditional	A.C. Arthur	$9.95
Until Death Do Us Part	Susan Paul	$8.95
Vows of Passion	Bella McFarland	$9.95
Wedding Gown	Dyanne Davis	$8.95
What's Under Benjamin's Bed	Sandra Schaffer	$8.95
When Dreams Float	Dorothy Elizabeth Love	$8.95
When I'm With You	LaConnie Taylor-Jones	$6.99
Whispers in the Night	Dorothy Elizabeth Love	$8.95
Whispers in the Sand	LaFlorya Gauthier	$10.95
Who's That Lady?	Andrea Jackson	$9.95
Wild Ravens	Altonya Washington	$9.95
Yesterday Is Gone	Beverly Clark	$10.95
Yesterday's Dreams, Tomorrow's Promises	Reon Laudat	$8.95
Your Precious Love	Sinclair LeBeau	$8.95

Order Form

Mail to: Genesis Press, Inc.
P.O. Box 101
Columbus, MS 39703

Name ______________________________
Address ______________________________
City/State ____________________ Zip ____________
Telephone ____________________

Ship to (if different from above)
Name ______________________________
Address ______________________________
City/State ____________________ Zip ____________
Telephone ____________________

Credit Card Information
Credit Card # ____________________ ☐ Visa ☐ Mastercard
Expiration Date (mm/yy) ____________ ☐ AmEx ☐ Discover

Qty.	Author	Title	Price	Total

Use this order form, or call 1-888-INDIGO-1

Total for books ____________
Shipping and handling:
$5 first two books,
$1 each additional book ____________
Total S & H ____________
Total amount enclosed ____________

Mississippi residents add 7% sales tax